THE HOUSE OF RODRIGUEZ

When schoolteacher Anna escapes to Spain for a holiday, sparks fly when a misunderstanding on her very first day there leads to confrontation with Isandro, an arrogant architect. Despite their initial falling out, she comes to know his sister Teresa and her children — though Isandro's girlfriend Maria is anything but welcoming. Gradually drawn into the warm, close-knit family, Anna even begins to thaw towards Isandro. But after the fallout of a past relationship, she is wary of ever opening her heart to anyone again . . .

WENDY KREMER

THE HOUSE OF RODRIGUEZ

Complete and Unabridged

LINFORD
Leicester

First published in Great Britain in 2013

First Linford Edition
published 2014

A catalogue record for this book is available
from the British Library.

ISBN 978–1–4448–2189–5

Published by
F. A. Thorpe (Publishing)
Anstey, Leicestershire

Set by Words & Graphics Ltd.
Anstey, Leicestershire
Printed and bound in Great Britain by
T. J. International Ltd., Padstow, Cornwall

This book is printed on acid-free paper

1

Anna arched her stiff body and laid her sketch pad aside. She shaded her eyes and gazed at the bluish-grey waters crashing onto the jagged rocks below. Beyond her, the Mediterranean Sea stretched to the horizon. Six whole weeks to relax!

When Anna mentioned she planned to go to Spain this summer, Mike told her about St. Sabatien. Today she thanked him silently for his tip. Mass tourism had not yet reached the small fishing village. Local vegetable farms employed most of its inhabitants these days, but there were still some brightly painted fishing boats in the harbour and the fishermen still repaired their nets in the sunshine.

The wind plastered her thin cotton blouse to her slim body. The temperature felt pleasant, the sun shone and the air was salty. She leaned back against the mottled rock. Her backbone settled into to a more comfortable position on the rough surface of the boulder. She threw her arms behind her head and stared up at the sky. Wisps of cloud wandered quietly inland across an otherwise clear blue heaven.

'May I ask what you're doing here?'

The deep voice startled her, and she jerked to a sitting position. 'Pardon?' A tall stranger stood astride a nearby rock looking down at her. Feeling flustered she scrambled awkwardly to her feet. She thought she'd be as tall but he was much taller. She looked up at his face: olive skin stretched over high cheek-bones and he had dark, probing eyes. He had one hand stuck in the pocket of his chinos. Although his clothes were casual in style, Anna decided he wasn't a fisherman or a run-of-the-mill employee. He spoke excellent English but with a slight accent. That, and his dark features, proclaimed he was Spanish.

He repeated, 'I asked you what you're doing here. This is my property. Trespassers are not welcome.'

Anna looked at him. She felt under attack and annoyed by the tone of his voice. Normally under similar circumstances, she would simply apologise and leave, but she resented his pushy attitude. 'Is it? I didn't see a warning sign.'

He frowned and his dark eyebrows formed a straight line. His expression still contained no vestige of sympathy. 'There is one, at the bottom of the rocks. You went past it when you came up. It's in Spanish, English and German; I presume you understand one of those languages?'

He sounded very confident. She wondered if he was right and she was wrong. Had she missed his pesky warning board? Anna was polite by nature, and she also aimed to stick to the rules. She understood why he'd be annoyed if strangers continually trespassed.

As casually as she could manage, she answered. 'Really? If that's true, then I apologise. I never trespass when there's a sign telling people to keep out.'

A sudden gust of wind swept her sketching pad along the surface of the rock. Before Anna could grab it, it slid over the edge and landed in a crevice at the base of the rocks. The rubber bands fixing the sheets snapped. The pages stayed in place but they rippled in the wind. She cursed. 'Damn it!' She glanced across to him again. 'Sorry! I don't usually swear either. I'll collect it on my way down.'

He considered her for a moment, and decided to be more courteous. 'Why did you come up here in the first place? If you were hoping to cross to the other side, it wasn't worth the bother. There are no cosy bays on the other side of my house. Tourism ends here. The rock-face all along this part of the coast is very steep. It's almost vertical in places and downright dangerous to climb.'

She met his glance. 'I wasn't looking

for another beach. I went for a walk along the beach when I arrived yesterday. The tide was out and I saw parts of your house. It's such an unusual design, in such a perfect position. It caught my eye. I decided to draw it this morning.' He still looked sceptical. Anna felt disappointed that her praise didn't pacify him.

'Why? Are you an architect?'

She brushed her ash-blonde hair out of her eyes and laughed softly. 'Heavens, no! I'm a primary school teacher on holiday, from the UK.' She added, 'Sketching is a hobby. I draw things of interest I see, and make my own book of personal memories.'

She couldn't tell if he believed her or not. He stared silently with an unreadable expression. He was Anna's stereotypical idea of what a Spaniard should look like. She itched to capture his features on paper. Give him a cape, and dress him in a matador's suit and pink socks and he'd be every woman's epitome of a bullfighter. She re-considered; he was too tall to be a bullfighter. She regarded his thin aristocratic features, high cheekbones, slender form and his arresting good looks. He was evidently plain-spoken by nature, and he stood as if he was lord of all he surveyed. She studied him too, and the longer she looked, the more she liked his angular, rugged features.

He gave her a brief nod as he listened to her explanation about her hobby. Anna hoped his hostility had faded. It hadn't. He said,

'Please don't come here again. I've avoided erecting fencing because I don't want to interfere with nature, but I'm losing patience because you're not the first person to ignore the sign. I'll have to devise a way to make the rocks impassable, without spoiling appearances.' He considered her with a sceptical expression and added, 'The rocks are on my property and I can do what I like with them. I'd prefer to leave things as they are, but if people keep ignoring my wishes, I'll have to find another solution.'

Anna's cheeks reddened. She decided to draw attention again to the possibility that he might be wrong. 'I definitely didn't pass any sign. What does it look like?'

'Like any sign. It's a board with writing on it.' He drawled mockingly, 'I'm sure you've seen one before; they are usually a square-shaped piece of wood with painted lettering.'

She didn't miss the sarcasm and glared back. 'Well, I didn't see yours. Where is it?'

He nodded. 'Down there; where the rocks begin.'

Anna picked up her straw hat, and grabbed her satchel and pencils. He clearly didn't want to believe her. He was unfriendly. There was no point in further discussion. She pronounced defiantly, 'Perhaps you should check if it's still there. Or put it in a more prominent position.'

Without waiting for a reply, Anna began the awkward decent. She made a detour and scrambled between the narrow crevices to recover her sketch-pad. She stuffed it into her satchel. Looking up, he was still watching. It looked like he'd wait until he was sure she'd left his property. Perhaps he was justified, but he should give people the benefit of the doubt. Anna concentrated on reaching the beach and grudgingly admitted that if people invaded his privacy too often, he was entitled to be angry and to doubt their excuses.

Once she reached the bottom of the rocks, she looked around for the board. She found it. It was lying face down in a pool between some rocks. She left it where it was and didn't look at the wording. She went back to tell him. His tall figure had disappeared.

Botheration! She'd looked forward to telling him she was right, and he was wrong. She hoisted her satchel to a more comfortable position and set off across the firm sands to her lodgings.

The small family hotel was down a side street near the harbour. By the time she reached the shady cobbled street, her annoyance had almost faded. His false accusation still irritated, and she wished she'd thought of asking him to show her the signboard. That would have made him feel uncomfortable!

Anna smiled a greeting at Señora Mendora, the wife of the hotel owner. She wore a wrap-around apron and was busy cleaning the reception area. Anna took the stairs two at a time and hurried down the corridor to her small bedroom with its casement window. Heavy, old-fashioned Spanish style furniture filled the room. The hotel was family-run and conventional, but the Mendoras were both warm-hearted and friendly. She ran the hotel; he cooked and did renovations and repairs. Anna loved the atmosphere and was glad she wasn't in one of the super-chic, anonymous hotels in the over-populated tourist resorts farther down the coast. She opened the window and the faint scent of bright red geraniums invaded the room and banished any lingering irritation. Forget him. She didn't intend him to spoil her stay in Spain.

* * *

He signed *Isandro Delgado Rodriquez* with a flourish at the bottom of the blueprint and stepped back to look at it. He studied the plan critically again and felt pleased. He'd included all his ideas and he knew they were good ones. He rolled it up stuck it in an oversize mailing tube and placed it with various other finished designs and blueprints on a side table. Franco could take everything back with him on Sunday and deliver his entry in plenty of time. The whole concept had been a challenge but the finished result looked almost better on paper than it had in his mind's eye.

He left the drawing board and went into the kitchen. The working surfaces and cupboards in the kitchen were a mixture of polished steel and wood.

When he furnished the house, he'd often used polished steel in the fittings and features. He liked the sleek surface and the smooth look. Exploring one of the cupboards, he found a long glass and proceeded to fill it with ice-cubes and Campari. He went out through the French windows in the living room onto the stone terrace. The leisure furniture remained there permanently, even in winter. At present, they had thick inviting cushions.

His glance drifted across the terrace to a slightly raised level and a trapeze-form swimming pool. The shape of the pool was integrated into the rough rock behind it. The bright turquoise colour of the water and the shades of rust-brown rock complimented each other perfectly. He took a sip and simply enjoyed his own creation. He'd had endless offers from people who wanted to buy the house, but he'd never sell. It would be like selling part of his soul. He strolled towards the balustrade facing the sea.

The hardy dwarf trees and plants bordering the edges gave it the feeling of a garden. He leaned on the metalwork and looked across the Mediterranean.

Looking at the rocks directly below, his thoughts returned to the girl. Her fine complexion, thick blonde hair and pale grey eyes confirmed her statement that she came from the UK. She had a good figure that curved in all the right places. Had she made up her excuse about not seeing a warning? Had she climbed the rocks despite seeing the sign, or had she genuinely not seen she was trespassing? He wondered if she was telling the truth. She didn't look like the type of girl who lied, but you never knew these days. He'd check it tomorrow, just in case. He didn't want to put visible barriers on the rocks, but he wanted his privacy. It looked like he needed to find a solution that would blend in with the surroundings.

The feel of the sun on his skin and the sea breezes ruffling his hair relaxed him completely. He looked at his watch and smiled. Teresa would be back with the children soon. The peace would then end. It had been an extra challenge to carry on with his work despite their presence. He concentrated on enjoying this moment. He'd been working non-stop for several days to meet the deadline.

The sun was on the decline. He ignored provoking thoughts, including the girl with her sketchpad.

* * *

After breakfast next morning, Anna packed her canvas satchel, and drove her hired car inland along a country road. She had no special destination and simply enjoyed the smell of grass and the look of the countryside as she drove along. She stopped after a while to visit a small ancient church in a sleepy village. The building was austere in its design, but the atmosphere and down-to-earth appearance wakened her interest. She made a quick sketch and dabbed matching colours down the side of the paper from her small paint-box. If she decided to paint the sketch later, her colour daubs would be a tangible help to get the shading right. The temperature was rising and she decided to return to the hotel. She looked forward to a cold drink and a shower. She had to get used to the vicinity so decided not to search for another cafe; it was easier to turn back to St. Sabatien.

She parked her hired car in an appointed spot, on the slope behind the hotel. Anna walked around the corner and sat at one of the three small bistro tables outside the hotel. Señora Mendora bustled out; her earrings jangled as she absent-mindedly wiped the table. She asked Anna what she wanted.

'Some orange juice, please.' Most of the local people understood and spoke a little English. It made her feel a little ashamed that she hadn't made an effort to learn some Spanish before she came.

2

A woman, in her thirties, sat with two small children at a neighbouring table. The little girl was chatty and pretty. The little boy looked a few years older. They both had bright eyes and black hair. The two children bickered about who'd chosen the best ice cream. Anna didn't need to understand the language to guess that. Their mother scolded them and gave Anna an apologetic look. Anna returned the smile and pulled out her sketching pad.

She flipped through the sketches while waiting for her drink. She liked some of them, and wrinkled her nose at others. The two children ate their ice creams quickly. Their mother wanted to enjoy her coffee in peace, so she gave them permission to leave the table when they finished. They sidled across to Anna and began to take furtive looks at her pictures.

Anna asked, 'Want to look?'

They obviously understood English because they nodded. Anna opened the sketchpad at the beginning. They began to turn the pages and chatter about the drawings in Spanish.

Their mother looked across. 'Don't let them bother you.'

Anna smiled. 'It's perfectly all right. I like children.'

Señora Mendora arrived with Anna's fresh orange juice.

The woman said, 'Let me pay for that.'

'Please! It's not necessary.'

'It is, as compensation for my nosy children.' She patted the seat next to her. 'That's if you think you can trust them alone with your pictures.'

Anna moved across and sat down. The other woman had hair the colour of raven's wings, and it was pinned in a smart chignon. Her clothes looked simple, but they were chic and clearly expensive. Pearl earrings and a thick silver bracelet finished off a fashionable and well-groomed appearance.

She held out her hand. 'Hello! My name is Teresa. Teresa Delgado Rodriquez de Arroyo.' She smiled at Anna's dazed expression. 'I know, Spanish names are a mouthful, aren't they? We automatically get the surname of our mother and father. When we marry we add our husband's name.'

Anna smiled. 'Oh, I see. My name is Anna Coleman. Anna.'

'That's much easier to remember.' She told Señora Mendora to add the juice to her bill. The landlady nodded, and disappeared again. 'I presume you're a visitor?'

Anna nodded. 'Yes. This is my first visit to Spain. Someone recommended St. Sabatien to me. He said it was unspoiled and lovely. It is.'

Teresa nodded. 'There aren't many fishing villages left between Barcelona and the French border any more. Mass tourism has replaced fishing communities. Hideous multi-story hotels plaster most of the coastline these days, or luxury homes for people who only live here for part of the year.'

'That's why I'm so pleased this one has survived, and is still so authentic.'

'Me too! I hope the villagers won't give in to temptation and start selling their cottages to speculators. Once investors have bought one or two, they demolish the houses and replace them with a flashy hotel. The second hotel follows the first, and then it'll end up an atrocious holiday centre, like everywhere else.'

A tall, slim man with chocolate-brown eyes, dark hair and an olive complexion targeted Teresa and interrupted their conversation. She beamed at him. 'Franco! What are you doing here? I didn't know you were coming.'

He took her shoulders and kissed her cheeks. 'Isandro told me you were here with the children. I decided to come to see you all. The designs for his museum complex in Sent Adrian are finished. You know that he's one of the contenders for the contract?' His sister nodded. 'I said I'd save him an extra trip and hand them in at the offices at beginning of next week. The place is just around the corner from my flat.'

'And? What are his chances?'

'Your guess is as good as mine. You know his designs are fantastic but costs are a deciding factor these days and Isandro refuses to cut corners.' He paused. 'Hey, why are we talking English?'

Teresa gestured towards Anna. 'Because I was talking to Anna when you arrived.'

He looked at Anna with interest. His white teeth flashed and he smiled at her.

'Anna is a visitor from the UK.'

His eyes twinkled as he held out his hand.

Teresa added, 'Anna this is Franco, my brother.' Franco held her hand longer than necessary.

'Hello Anna.'

Anna smiled up at him. 'Hello!'

The two children interrupted them. They came back with Anna's sketch-pad. They sounded surprised and excited. 'Look Mama, Uncle Isandro's house.'

They put the pad on the table and everyone considered the half-finished picture.

Teresa commented, 'Good heavens, yes. That's *Casa Grande*. When did you do that?'

Franco added, 'You've caught the basic lines perfectly. It's good.'

Anna felt pleased. 'I climbed the rocks yesterday to sketch it but I didn't finish it because the owner came out and chased me off. He said I was trespassing. Do you know him?'

Teresa laughed. 'Very well! He's Isandro, my other brother.'

Startled by the information, Anna recovered quickly enough to add, 'I honestly didn't see the '*Keep Out*' sign where he told me it was. I found it later. It was face down, in a rock pool.'

'Oh, dear. And Isandro thought you were intruding?'

Franco laughed softly. 'I bet he didn't mince his words.'

'He wasn't exactly rude, but he did wait to make sure I'd left before he left himself.'

The two laughed. Teresa explained, 'He moved here recently. His house caused a minor sensation in the beginning because the people in the village thought it was the beginning of the end. When they realized that the house was barely visible, and that he didn't intend to encourage anyone else to do anything similar, they accepted him. I think he's even on local committees now, about environmental issues.'

Tilting her head to the side, Anna remarked, 'That's fast progress. Especially when you realized he's already changed the environment here by building his house where it is.'

Franco burst out laughing.

Anna hurried to add, 'Admittedly, it is well-hidden, so the basic look of the village hasn't changed. It must be difficult for a small community to resist the attraction of money and big business these days. Money talks, doesn't it?'

'From what Isandro tells us, it looks like local people are determined to keep the speculators out. They fight to have their say in decisions that affect the area. The local planning department is on their side and they've already made useful connections to higher authorities. Nowadays people don't want to repeat past mistakes. It makes them unpopular and they don't want to lose their jobs. Isandro knows about regulations, constructions, pitfalls, and problems. He can argue a case and talk knowledgably. People around here appreciate that.'

Anna nodded. 'If he is an architect, I expect he can soon see the advantages and the disadvantages.'

Teresa looked at her watch and then at her brother. 'Are you on your way home? If so, I'll pay for our drinks and we'll come with you.'

He nodded. 'I need to buy some cake on the way, because Isandro just said he'd cook us the meal this evening, but I have to contribute the dessert.'

Teresa hurried the children along. 'It was lovely to meet you Anna. I hope we'll meet again. I'll tell my brother that he got it all wrong and you weren't trespassing.'

'Don't bother, it's not important. It was nice to meet you all.' She picked up her sketchbook and gave the two children an extra, 'Bye!'

The children nodded and smiled. Franco gave her a generous smile. 'I hope to see you again, Anna. Enjoy your stay!'

★　★　★

Anna leaned back contentedly after a delicious meal. She circled the red Spanish wine in her glass and studied the star-studded heavens. The hotel served the evening meal in the inner courtyard whenever possible. It was an ideal place with lots of greenery and an ornate fountain bubbling in the centre.

The hotel only had six rooms. At present, Anna and an elderly couple from Norwich were the only occupants. She'd heard the other rooms were booked from the coming weekend. The elderly English couple exchanged pleasantries with Anna but went out for a walk straight after their meal.

Anna thought about whether to order another glass of wine, or if a bottle would be cheaper in the long run. Señora Mendora came looking for her.

'Telephone, Miss Coleman.'

'For me?' She was puzzled. She hadn't even given her parents the hotel number yet, or told them she'd arrived safely.

Señora Mendora bustled around the tables, clearing the dishes tidying the tablecloths and adjusting the chairs.

Anna went into the small lobby. The telephone lay abandoned on the reception desk. She picked it up.

'Hello, Anna Coleman.'

'Miss Coleman, this is Isandro Rodriquez. You met my sister and

24

brother this afternoon?'

Her eyebrows lifted and she wondered what he wanted. 'Yes, I met them briefly. What can I do for you?'

He paused. 'I want to apologise. My sister told me the sign was lying in the sand. I just checked and it was.'

'Yes, I know. I came back to tell you, but you'd already disappeared.'

'Would you like to join us for a drink, to make amends?'

Anna longed to see the house's interior, and she'd enjoy meeting Teresa and Franco again, but the prospect of seeing Isandro Rodriquez again irritated her 'Thanks, that's kind of you, but I already have an appointment this evening.'

'Oh.' He sounded surprised. 'Another time perhaps?'

'Perhaps. Say hello to Teresa and Franco, please. Thank you for calling. Goodnight Señor Rodriquez.'

There was a moment of silence and then he said, 'Goodnight.'

She wondered if she'd been sensible

to refuse. She didn't even know what Spanish customs were about accepting or rejecting harmless invitations to a glass of wine. Perhaps she'd just committed a faux pas. Even if he'd been ungracious yesterday, at least he'd tried to put things right today. She estimated he was someone who didn't do anything unless he chose to. She recalled the strong lines of his chin and how determined and tenacious he seemed.

★   ★   ★

She went upstairs to find her parents' telephone number. Her brother had emigrated to Australia five years ago. He'd married an Australian girl and they were expecting their first baby. Mum and Dad had decided to visit them and they were having a wonderful time. She'd already spoken to them before she left for her holiday.

She picked up her mobile with its stored numbers and grabbed the telephone card she'd bought that morning. Telephoning from a public telephone box was cheaper than the hotel or her cell phone. She noticed a box near the harbour this morning. She'd met a Swedish girl coming out of it who'd explained how she got an overseas connection.

Mum and Dad sounded thrilled as they talked about the country and the people they'd met so far. Her Mum asked, 'Have you given it some serious thought yet, love?'

Looking across at the harbour blanketed in shadows, she answered, 'Not really, but I will, I promise. Just thinking about what it would entail makes my mind boggle.'

'It's up to you, love. We won't push, promise.' They talked for a while. Anna told them about St. Sabatien. They told her what they'd seen recently. After staying with her brother and his wife for a while, her parents were now travelling to see some of the country. They chatted until the money ran out.

Returning to the hotel, a jeep containing Teresa, Franco and Isandro passed her. Franco was at the wheel and he beeped. Startled, she automatically waved and watched it disappear around the next corner. She'd told Isandro Rodriquez she had something better to do this evening. He now realized that she'd made an excuse not to accept his invitation. She felt uncomfortable with the thought.

3

She met Teresa and the children again, at the end of the same week while sketching some fishing boats from one of the bistro tables outside a pavement cafe. The little boy, Eduardo, noticed her and tugged at his mother's dress. Teresa came across.

'Morning Anna.' She glanced at the half-finished drawing. 'Still at it?' She eyed an empty chair. 'May I join you?'

Anna smiled. 'Yes, of course. I just love drawing and painting. During the school term I don't have time for it, apart from scenery for school events, etc.'

'I wish I had your talent.' Teresa gave the children permission to go to watch the activity in the harbour. 'Stay away from the edge! I don't want to jump in to save you, my dress cost too much.' They scurried off.

Anna put her pencil aside.

'You're a teacher?'

'Um! I studied art and I then decided I'd like to work with children, so I had to get extra qualifications but it paid off. I love teaching.'

'It's not everyone's dream job — to be shut up in a room with small children all day.'

'Well I like it.' Anna enquired curiously, 'And you're visiting your brother? On holiday?'

'It's a bit of a forced holiday. My husband is in the diplomatic service. At present, he's in some unpronounceable country. He specialises in economics, mostly assessing pros and cons for prospective investors. Sometimes we can go with him, sometimes not. It depends on the working environment and how risky the place is.'

'It sounds like a precarious job, but also very interesting. How do the children get their schooling?'

'Either there's a suitable school within easy travelling distance, or I take lessons with us and they have home schooling. When we're home in Madrid, they go to an international school. If there's a safety risk, I stay in Madrid. In the school holidays, I visit my parents or Isandro if I need a change of scenery. Franco only has a small one-bedroom flat in the centre of Barcelona so I don't bother him much. I'm lucky that my family is so supportive. When the children are older they'll need advanced schooling and the chance to make lasting friendships. Then it'll be a choice between them and my husband. I'm not looking forward to that. At the moment I can't imagine leaving them behind.'

'They seem to be well-balanced, intelligent children. Life isn't always straightforward, is it?'

A waiter came and Teresa ordered a coffee. 'If I had to leave them, my parents would take them. But that's not like a short visit. It wouldn't be fair on them.'

Anna took a sip of water. 'If they say they can cope, they probably can. What about a good boardingschool? They could board during the week and go to your parents for the weekend. If you make enquiries about a school's reputation in the right places, you'll soon find a good one. The children might even enjoy it, once they've settled down. Children are more adaptable than you think. Your children know your husband's work makes staying together difficult, so they won't feel jettisoned. If they're at the same school, they'd support each other, and seeing their grandparents every weekend would give them a sense of security.'

'Isandro suggested something similar. I don't know if there's a good boarding school within travelling distance of my parents.' She ran her fingers through her loose hair. 'Perhaps I worry too much. Sometimes my husband's posting is somewhere civilized. Are you married? I take it that you're not; otherwise, you wouldn't be here on your own. On the other hand, couples these days often spend holidays apart, don't they.'

Anna shook her head. 'No. I'm single. My parents say I'm too choosy.'

Teresa's coffee arrived. She stirred the creamy surface with a silver spoon and said, 'Believe me when you see how fast some people's marriages land on the rocks, you can never be too choosy. By the way, you surprised Isandro yesterday. I think he expected you to jump at the chance of joining us for a glass of wine.'

'Did he? I trespassed and he apologised. I thought that was enough.'

She laughed softly. 'Isandro doesn't like being in the wrong. He doesn't often make mistakes. He found the sign yesterday evening and put it back this morning. At breakfast he was going on about fixing thick metal cables attached to rings on the rock and hanging a printed metal sign!'

'It was a mistake. It's not important.'

Teresa swept her windblown hair off

her face. 'He's our family's sandwich-kid. I'm older and a girl, so I was forgiven if I got into trouble. Franco is younger, and his sins were forgiven because he was 'little'. Isandro often covered for us and sometimes took the blame for what we did. It helped form his character. Today he steers clear of people if they come too close or grow too demanding.' She lifted her cup and took a sip. 'It also made him determined and self-confident.'

The two of them sat chatting for a while. Anna told her about her family and about her school. Teresa explained she lived in a flat near the centre of Madrid and loved reading and keeping fit.

★ ★ ★

Every day, Anna drove to somewhere new mentioned in her guidebook. She always avoided areas near the plastic-covered fruit and vegetables fields. Even though the work provided local people with employment, it ruined appearances.

She visited churches, old monasteries, church squares, and Roman remains — anything of interest described in the travel guide. One morning she decided to spend it on the beach. The sun blazed down and she bought some fruit from the market place on the way. Sauntering along with nothing on her mind, she stopped when someone called her name. A jeep with Franco and Isandro pulled in further along the road. Franco jumped out and came towards her.

His brown eyes twinkled. He beamed and said, 'Hello, Anna. I hoped to see you again. How are you?'

Anna felt flattered and smiled back. 'I'm fine, and how are you?' She looked briefly at Isandro sitting behind the steering wheel. He nodded and she nodded back. He stared straight ahead and she remembered how Teresa labelled him as reserved and stand-offish.

Franco said. 'Now that we've met, I feel great. How about sharing a meal with me one evening?'

Why should she refuse? She liked his happy-go-lucky, cheery attitude. Why shouldn't she go out with a Spaniard? 'Yes.'

'Good, a woman who knows her own mind. When? This evening? Alternative is Saturday.'

She noticed Isandro studying his watch out of the corner of her eye. 'This evening would be lovely. I haven't planned anything.'

'Well you have now.' He gave her dazzling smile; his white teeth contrasted nicely with his olive skin. 'Eight o'clock?'

Anna nodded.

Isandro was clearly impatient for Franco's return.

'I'll pick you up. You're staying with the Mendoras, aren't you?'

'Yes.'

'Till later then?' He jumped back into the jeep.

Isandro drove off without any leave-taking, and Anna watched the jeep disappear.

* * *

Anna chose a dress patterned in obscure forms. She'd only worn it a couple of times and a warm Spanish evening suited the light, flimsy material to perfection. Brushing her fair hair back behind her ears, she added long silver earrings as a final touch. She waited for him in the small hallway. He arrived dead on time.

'You look very chic.'

'Thank you!'

He offered his arm. 'I've booked at a restaurant on the edge of town. I thought we could walk there. It gives us more time to talk.'

His white shirt fitted snugly and he wore well-cut chinos. St. Sabatien seemed a sleepy place at this time of day. The narrow side-streets were almost empty. Anna's sandals echoed on the sidewalk. Lanterns glowed softly. The smell of flowers and the sea wafted on the warm air. Anna soon found her first impressions about him were

correct. Franco's nature was full of
sunshine, like the land he came from.
She relaxed and hoped he realized she
wasn't looking for a holiday romance.
Franco's looks reminded her more of
Teresa than of Isandro.

When they reached the restaurant,
she loved it. It only had a handful of
tables. Checked cloths covered the
tables and candles flickered in pro-
tected wind-lights in the centre. His
company and the food were faultless.
He was very relaxed, laughed a lot, and
kept up a light enjoyable form of
flirtation. Perhaps Spanish men were
more confident when they dated
someone for the first time. Few British
men of her acquaintance would have
approached a first date in exactly the
same light-hearted way. During the
conversation, Isandro's name automatically cropped up and she learned he
had a girlfriend who was a presenter
with regional television. She wasn't
nationally famous yet, but Franco
believed that was a matter of time. She

was making connections with the right people.

Anna couldn't help asking, 'Does she live here?'

Franco shook his head. 'In Barcelona. She usually visits on the weekend, if her work allows, or he comes to Barcelona. She needs the limelight. Isandro needs peace to be creative.'

'They sound like opposites, but sometimes opposites attract.'

Franco shrugged. 'I've often wondered where the attraction lies, because they're two different personalities. Isandro's introverted and Maria is a firework.' He grinned. 'Perhaps things level out in the bedroom. They've been together for two or three months now.'

For some reason, Anna wanted to ignore the idea of Isandro Rodriguez in bed.

When they strolled back, they lingered for a few minutes by the harbour wall. The breeze plastered her dress to her body and messed her hair.

She asked, 'Are you an architect too?'

The wind buffeted his hair and the warmth of his smile echoed in his voice. 'No. I studied engineering, and I help to coordinate various projects in a small company employed by the city authorities. It's interesting, and the company's doing well. Isandro is the creative one in our family.'

'Engineering is creative too, isn't it?'

'Perhaps, but you don't look at a pump station or a rubbish dump, and go *Wow* do you?'

'But everyone needs water and rubbish disposal. Some aspects of life need to be practical.'

'Everyone needs beauty to look at too, and his buildings are beautiful. The present project he's working on is a museum extension. Only a handful of architects were asked to submit ideas. The administration is just around the corner from my flat. I'm actually here to see Teresa and the kids. Submissions have to be in by Monday, next week, and as it doesn't matter who delivers them, I offered to save him a trip. If he surmounts the first hurdle, he has to handle the rest personally of course.'

Anna brushed strands of hair out of her face and watched the lights dancing on the water in the harbour. 'If his designs are anything like his house, they'll be good.'

'Yes, *Casa Grande* is great, isn't it? Everyone thought that the rocky foundation would block any real development. He got round that.' With pride, he added, 'I helped him with some of the technicalities. People envy him the house. You should see the inside; you'd love it.'

Anna didn't think that was likely any more. Isandro Rodriguez and Anna Coleman didn't gel. The idea annoyed her because she generally got on well with most people. Their first encounter went badly and things hadn't improved. 'From the side it's quite impressive.'

'Isandro will make it to the top one day, because he has vision and he doesn't compromise. Many budding

41

architects end up doing run-of-the-mill stuff because they want money fast. Isandro follows a slower path, but he climbs continually.'

'He must be earning plenty of money if he could afford to build that house.'

'Appearances deceive! He's no jet-setter. The bank lent him money to build it because he convinced them it would be a good investment and they'd get their money back fast. He didn't merely build himself a house; he wanted a platform to show what he can do. Most visitors go away impressed and wanting something similar.'

She laughed softly. 'A sort of 3D visiting card? Very far-sighted.'

'Now and then he gives a cocktail party for the right people, the ones with money. He'll stop doing that one day, but such events bring him lots of other commissions. The house made the pages of a glossy magazine once, and that stirred a lot of interest and brought work. He has plenty to do these days.'

Anna mused that the Rodriguez

family were all very interesting people. Their parents could be proud of all their children.

They sauntered back to the hotel. He took Anna's hand and kissed it in an old-fashioned gesture, and then kissed her cheek. She was glad. He sensed she didn't want a holiday romance, or a one-night-stand. She liked his charming, amorous attitude. He didn't storm the barricades and adjusted his strategy to suit his partner.

'Goodnight Anna. I hope we'll do this again.'

'Thank you for a lovely evening. I really enjoyed it.'

'My pleasure. Sleep well.' His white teeth flashed in the shadows. He kissed her on her cheek again and she didn't resist.

'You too! Night!' Anna turned and went indoors.

4

Leaning over the low wall, Anna studied the small beach. On the weekend, people plastered the sands. Today it was much quieter. She spotted Eduardo and Ina playing with kites near the edge of the sea. Teresa sat on a rug near the seawall. She waved when she saw Anna, patted the rug beside her, and beckoned. Somehow, it felt good to meet someone she knew in such foreign surroundings. Anna skipped down the step and joined her. Flopping down, she said,

'Hello. I see the children are enjoying themselves.'

* * *

Teresa didn't look well. Her face was ashen and her eyes were full of strain.

'Yes. They can play and swim up at

44

the house, but the terrace is too small for them to run around very much, so sometimes we come down to the beach.'

Anna looked at her more closely. 'I hope you don't mind me saying so, but you look off colour. Is anything wrong?'

'I think I've eaten something that doesn't agree with me. I've had stomachache since early this morning. It's getting worse, not better.'

'Does anyone else in the family feel the same way?'

'No, only me. That doesn't mean much though. It could be something that we'll develop, one after the other.'

'Well, it can't be fun for you to sit in the sun if you don't feel well.' Anna glanced at the children. 'Why don't you leave them with me for a few hours? You can go home and lie down. You can fetch them later, when you're feeling better, or I'll bring them home if you like.'

Teresa's face brightened. 'You wouldn't mind? That would be great. To be honest,

I feel rotten. A little rest with a hot water bottle might do the trick. I hoped it would disappear as fast as it came. So far, there's no diarrhoea, but perhaps that's still to come. I'm sure the children wouldn't mind staying with you. They like you.' She shouted and beckoned to Ina and Eduardo.

The children came running, dragging their kites through the sand. Teresa explained that Anna had offered to look after them for a while because she wanted to go home to lie down. The pair of them eyed Anna cautiously but then they both smiled and nodded.

Teresa reached out for her bag. 'They understand English, and they speak it quite well too considering their age. That's one great advantage of an international school. The main teaching language is English. If they get on your nerves, just bring them back home.' She spoke to the children in Spanish. 'Behave yourselves! If Anna tells me you didn't listen there'll be trouble.'

The two of them nodded dutifully.

Getting to her feet, she looked at Anna. 'You're sure? If I didn't feel so rotten I wouldn't dump them on you like this. Isandro is visiting a building site; he's not due back for a couple of hours otherwise he could take over.'

'Honestly, it's no trouble. Go home and relax.'

'I will. Thank you! I'll call at the chemist's on the way. Perhaps he'll give me something to help. The children's towels and their stuff are in that bag.'

Anna nodded. 'Off you go. We'll be fine.'

Teresa gave the children a quick hug, brushed the sand from her colourful beach dress and fought her way up the stone steps on to the small promenade.

The children waited until she reached the top and turned to wave cheerio.

Anna said, 'Let's get your kites up and flying again. It looked like you'd almost succeeded when your mum called you. The winds are stronger near the water, so let's go back to where you were a few minutes ago.'

Any shyness melted away when she helped them to get their colourful kites back up into the air. Once they were sailing far above them, the kites rose and fell in audible swoops. They all enjoyed the struggle to stay in control and keep them flying. They giggled and larked about like any other children at the seaside. Anna loved the fun almost as much as the children did.

* * *

Anna was very familiar with how erratic children's interests could be sometimes. After they'd flown kites for a while, she encouraged them to build an impressive sand castle and it kept them busy for quite a time. Then they all went looking for ice cream. Fortified, Ina chose some postcards for Anna to send to some friends and Eduardo acted as interpreter when they bought stamps from the local post office. Anna checked her watch. It was nearly four o'clock, and the children looked tired and hungry.

She decided to take them home. Perhaps Teresa was waiting for them, or she'd fallen asleep and lost track of the time.

Anna took charge of their kites and the children shouldered their respective beach bags. They strolled back along the promenade and up the road around the slight bend until they reached Isandro's house. From the roadway, the driveway of natural polished rock ended at the front door. The house was two cube-shaped buildings, one of them jutting out beyond the other to fuse with the copper and tan surface of the rock. The children raced to the entrance and rang the bell. They waited impatiently. By the time Anna reached them, they'd already tried several times, in vain.

Shading their eyes, they peered through the thin strips of smoked glass right and left of the doorway, hoping to see some movement within, but everything remained silent and stationary. Anna rang the bell again. Something must be wrong. Teresa loved her children too much to ignore them. Climbing the rocks and trying to check the house from the side would be risky. She decided there must be a logical explanation but it was silly to wait here in the sun. She searched her bag for pencil and paper, and wrote, *'Taken the children back to the hotel. — Anna'*. She put it under a large pebble directly in front of the door. The children looked apprehensive; they couldn't understand why their mother wasn't at home.

She tried to sound cheerful. 'We'll go back to my hotel. Your Mum will turn up soon, I'm sure. Perhaps she went shopping in the village and our paths crossed.'

They still looked troubled but they followed Anna without a protest.

* * *

She kept them busy with paper and pencil and Señora Mendora supplied lemonade and almond biscuits. The inner courtyard provided a peaceful haven as the heat of the day began to weaken. Anna was in the process of suggesting the children might like to go up to her room when she heard Isandro's voice. Ina and Eduardo abandoned their drawings and ran to him. He ruffled their heads and turned to Anna. He looked austere but she'd never seen him laugh so his expression didn't suggest anything out of the ordinary had happened.

She noticed his square jaw tense. 'Thanks for looking after them.'

Watching him, she noted there was edginess in his facial expression and his voice. 'No problem, they are both very good. I took them back to your house about four this afternoon but no one answered the doorbell. Is Teresa home?'

He turned to the children. 'Collect your stuff and we'll leave straight away.' They rushed to the table, relieved that someone had come to take them home at last. He then turned to Anna and ran his hand down his face. 'Thanks! I found your message. Teresa had already phoned me to tell me they were with you when she was on her way to hospital.'

Anna's eyes widened. 'Hospital? What happened?'

'You know she had a stomachache?'

Anna nodded. 'I met them all on the beach this morning and she told me she wasn't well. I suggested it might get better if went home to rest for a while.'

'When she left you, she went to the chemist. He thought it might be more than a stomach upset and sent her to a doctor. He diagnosed acute appendicitis and insisted she went straight to hospital. On the way, Teresa phoned me to give me the name of the clinic. I detoured from where I was at building site and went straight to the hospital.'

Anna's eyebrows lifted. 'Is everything okay?'

He gave an impatient shrug. 'They already had her in the operating theatre by the time I got there. Her appendix would probably have burst if she'd waited much longer. I stayed until I could speak to the surgeon and then I saw her briefly. She was very groggy, but she was glad to see me and worried about the children.' He spoke more to himself than to her. 'Once I've given them something to eat and they've had a shower, I'll take them with me. I can't leave them on their own.'

'Thank goodness that she went to the chemist and he thought it could be something more serious than stomach ache.'

'Yes, it was probably life-saving! I don't know if he actually suspected appendicitis, but it looks like it. I've already phoned Teresa's husband; he's on tenterhooks now and waiting for me to give him a progress report.'

'She's going to be all right, isn't she?' He nodded. Anna didn't think twice. 'Let me look after the children. It's not a good idea for you to take them with you tonight. Teresa might still feel very shaky or even under sedation. I think it would be better for them to see her tomorrow.'

His serious expression gradually softened into one of relief. 'That would be a great help. I tried to contact my cleaning lady on my way here; she's out. I haven't lived here long enough to know many people very well. The children know you so I'm sure they'll feel happy with you.'

'I'll see if Señora Mendora can put up an extra bed in my room.' She made a move, but he stopped her. The feel of his large hand on her bare skin sharpened her awareness of him. She told herself not to be ridiculous.

He studied her pale eyes and concerned expression. 'There's no need for that. They'll feel much happier up at the house. You can choose an empty guest room in the lower level. By the way, I'm Isandro. You're Anna?'

Anna nodded. 'Would you like me to tell the children about Teresa?'

He shook his head. 'No, I'll do that. Perhaps you can collect whatever you need overnight?'

She nodded and left. On the way, she met Señora Mendora and told her what had happened.

The children looked lost and upset when she returned. Anna crouched down. 'Your mum feels better already, but she's very tired and you'll have to wait until tomorrow morning to visit her. Your uncle will check that she's still okay and come straight back. I'll stay with you until then, if you'll let me.'

With misty eyes and quivering lips, Ina nodded. Anna wrapped her arms around the little girl. Eduardo tried to be brave but his sister infected him and he began to look just as nervous and lost. Anna handed Isandro her bag and took the children's hands in hers. 'I need your help to find everything.'

Isandro followed them, loaded with the bags and the kites. Out in the street, they all bundled into his jeep. Anna sat in the back with Ina on her lap. Isandro drove through the village and stopped outside the house. He unloaded everything.

He freed his key from his key ring. 'Here. I won't stop. The children know where everything is. I'll use Teresa's key when I come back. It's with her things at the hospital.'

Anna took it and their fingers touched. They stared across the shadows.

His face looked gaunt and unfathomable. 'Thanks again for helping.'

She blinked hard and replied, 'No thanks needed. Give Teresa my love, and love from the children too of course.'

He climbed with accustomed ease back into the jeep. They stood and watched him as he reversed out of the driveway and turned in the direction of the village. Anna concentrated on the children. They needed consolation. Fitting the key into the lock, she opened the door and they went inside. Eduardo reached for the switch the hallway was flooded with light.

5

Eduardo and Ina weren't hungry and Anna didn't force them to eat. Although the knowledge that their mum was in hospital, and they were tired from the day's happenings, it still took a long time until they agreed to go to bed. Anna chose an unoccupied guest room next door to them. The floor-length windows looked out across the sea. She saw ships, tiny spots of moving lights, far out in the Mediterranean. She went to bed, leaving her door ajar in case one of the children called. She woke abruptly when she heard movement upstairs. She looked at the bedside alarm clock. It was two a.m. She listened to sounds from the kitchen. Somehow, she knew it was him. She turned over and went back to sleep again.

Anna joined everyone at the breakfast table on the terrace. The children were chirpy again because they were going to see their mother after breakfast.

Facing Isandro across the table was a curious feeling, because she knew he guarded his privacy so carefully. Sharing breakfast with a stranger was breaking his attempts to safeguard just that. He gave her a slow smile when she joined them and it transformed his appearance. She felt almost buoyant when she viewed his face.

He asked, 'Did you sleep okay?'

'Yes, thanks. Very well.'

'Coffee or tea?' He gestured to the vacuum pots and the other items on the table. 'Help yourself!'

Munching on a bread roll with strong white teeth, he said, 'Teresa can come home in a couple of days. They don't keep anyone in hospital these days without a very good a reason.'

The children finished and said they

wanted to draw some pictures to take with them to the hospital. Isandro gave them permission to go. They disappeared into the house. For a moment, silence reigned.

'Who wants to be in hospital unless it's absolutely necessary?' She buttered a piece of toast and drank some coffee. Lifting her cup, she said, 'This is good. Coffee sets me up for the day.'

'I can't claim any credit; it comes from a coffee machine! I'm glad you like the taste.'

Anna looked across beyond the table towards the open sea. 'Your house is perfect. I'm sure people have told you so many times before. You're hidden away and very private, aren't you?'

He said in a matter-of-fact tone. 'Yes, as long as I can keep inquisitive visitors from climbing the rocks!' With a wry expression, he added, 'By the way, I'm really sorry I accused you of intentionally ignoring the sign and climbing the rocks up to the house. Privacy is always one of my main aims.'

She could forgive and forget. 'That's okay. You've already apologised about that.' She took a bite of toast and gestured around her. 'I was wondering how you managed to build the rooms. Was the rock already level enough and the right shape?'

He shook his head. 'We dynamited the rock down to the right depth to build a two-level house. I don't suppose local people liked me much when that happened, but we tried to get it done as fast as possible.'

'Well, the result was worth it.' She eyed him and asked carefully. 'Do you need help with the children until Teresa comes home? I'm willing to hang around. Just let me know. It's no trouble. They can come with me on my outings; they might even enjoy them. They're good company.'

He viewed her silently for a moment. 'That's very kind of you and I may be glad of your offer. My housekeeper isn't young, and children can be demanding. I'll manage to take care of them as long as nothing special needs my attention on one of my sites. My parents have offered to come, but my father is still working, and my mother can't drive. I'd have to pick her up from Barcelona. I don't think it's worth the hassle. I told her to wait until the weekend. Oh, would you mind packing Teresa a bag before we leave? You've a better idea of what she needs than I do. I expect she'll be out of bed today, so she'll need some leisure clothes.'

'Of course.'

'I would hate to spoil your holiday, but I may be glad of your help in an emergency.'

'You won't spoil my holiday. Eduardo and Ina are very well behaved.' Without thinking, she added, 'Anyway I'm doing it for Teresa, not for you.' She wished she hadn't said it; it came out all wrong. Not as she intended.

He straightened and wiped his mouth with the serviette. A veiled calmness showed in his eyes. 'Of course. I'm sure she'll be very grateful.'

She hurried to make good, but could tell from his expression that she'd sabotaged any progress they'd made. He probably thought their initial meeting on the rocks had completely ruined her opinion about him. For some reason she didn't want him to pigeonhole her as an unsympathetic hellcat. She added hurriedly, 'Taking them with me will be fun for me too. I'd like to, if they agree.' She changed direction and remarked. 'You've a lot of interesting sculptures and drawings. There's one that looks like a Picasso on the living-room wall.'

He answered politely, 'It not only looks like one, it is one.'

'Good heavens. Honestly?'

Still rather stiffly, he explained. 'I found it in a French flea market years ago. I bought it on instinct. The price was so ridiculous I knew I couldn't lose. I found it jumbled up among a pile of run-of-the-mill sketches. I had the devil's own luck that no one else spotted it before me. I've had it valued by an expert. It's authentic. It's not worth a fortune like one of his pictures, but it's worth a great deal more than I paid for it.'

'What a lucky find! How many people can say they own a Picasso? I like it. It reminds me of similar sketches I saw in the Picasso Museum in Paris. I bet whoever sold it has chewed his knuckles down to the bone by now.'

He stared at her appraisingly. 'I doubt it, because the stallholder either hadn't checked his stock or he guessed its origins wrongly. When I paid him, he didn't quibble and he didn't look at it closely, even then. Some of my other sculptures and drawings are worth more than when I bought them, but the Picasso sketch tops the list.' He hastened to add, 'I don't buy for investment purposes; I buy something because I like the look of it.'

Trying to sound friendlier, she said, 'Well you've a good eye, good taste and I think the design of your house is fantastic. That's probably why I wanted to draw *Casa Grande* in the first place. It is quite special.'

She thought her efforts were in vain. He studied her for a moment and then at last his voice held more warmth again.

'Thank you. I think so too.'

6

Anna thought that his independent character might get in the way of him asking her to take the children off his hands for a while — especially after her remark about wanting to help Teresa, and not him. It did. She heard nothing more until she decided she'd visit Teresa at the hospital one afternoon. She'd call at *Casa Grande*, and offered to take the children along with her.

She heard sounds of the children's laughter from inside on her arrival. When he opened the door, he looked ruffled but very relaxed. He stuffed his white shirt into the back of his washed-out jeans. Like most Spaniards, he clearly loved children. From the sounds of enjoyment, Eduardo and Ina loved him too.

She explained why she'd called. 'I thought Teresa might be glad of an extra visitor.'

'I took them with me this morning but I'm sure they'd love to come with you again. Teresa can't see them often enough either.' He gestured inside. 'Come in and you can ask them yourself.'

The children shouted their agreement boisterously and rushed off to find their shoes. His eyebrows lifted and he gave her a lopsided smile. Anna sensed however much he loved them, he was also glad to be free for a while. He explained how to get to the hospital while they waited for the children.

*   *   *

Teresa was delighted to see Anna and the children again. They sat outside in a shady green area belonging to the hospital. Teresa looked fine and Anna could tell she was already impatient to leave.

*   *   *

Encouraged by her success the previous day, she called again.

Filling the entrance with his build and height, Isandro considered her closely for a moment, before he invited her in.

She shook her head and juggled with her car keys. Something about him attracted her and she wanted to avoid complications. She was on holiday. Every time she saw him, her interest grew and that wasn't good. 'I wondered if the children would like to come on a trip. I told them yesterday I'm going to visit the remains of a Roman villa, and they said they'd never been there.'

With his hand on the doorframe, his eyes were full of hidden hope. 'That would be fantastic. There's an unexpected emergency at one of the sites. I was about to ask my housekeeper to come.'

'No need. If they'd like to come with me, I'll take them. We can always go somewhere else if they don't fancy Roman history. What time will you be back?'

'Is six o'clock okay with you? That'd give me time to visit a second site en route. I can give that a miss and come back earlier if you like.'

She lifted her hand in mid-air and waved his concern aside. 'No, go ahead. It's no problem! I'll wait in the car. Tell them to hurry up!' He turned away and she went back to her car.

She soon heard excited voices as he hurried the children along.

* * *

They set off, and she gave them some information about the remains of the Roman villa she'd read about in her guidebook. They found the place, down a narrow lane and off the main highway. It roused the children's fantasies and they all felt transported back in history. The villa was large and impressive, with beautiful floors and a mass of remaining foundations and walls. Anna bought them a children's book about the villa from the site kiosk. It also contained information about Roman settlements throughout Spain.

They read it to her while they sat at a shady table and drank lemonade. Just looking at the pictures while they read, Anna pretended to understand their Spanish. They had an enjoyable day.

★   ★   ★

Isandro felt that mere thanks weren't enough, because he stopped off on his way back from the hospital the following day. Señora Mendora phoned her from reception. He waited in the lobby and the sight of him filled her thoughts for a moment. The feeling confused her. He was nothing to her; just Teresa's brother, a mere acquaintance.

His dark chocolate eyes met her questioning grey ones. 'The children and I want to invite you for a meal, if you've nothing special planned.'

Anna had pigeonholed him as reserved, but his formality also made him different from most other men she'd met. She liked him. He was someone who thought things through before speaking or acting. She'd heard him laughing with the children and they told her that he played super games. He was a complex personality. He kept his cards close to his chest and only showed the world what he wanted them to see.

His unexpected invitation softened her opinion even more. Anna wondered if he thought she'd refuse. 'That's kind of you. I'd like that.'

He didn't sound surprised. 'Good. Come whenever you like. I've bought some steak.'

'Where are the children?'

'Outside in the jeep.' He lifted his hand and turned on his heel. 'See you later. Come whenever you're ready.'

* * *

She spent more time than necessary on her appearance and chose a silver-coloured sleeveless top and a favourite summer knee-length skirt. If he noticed her special effort, he didn't comment. Anna compared him and Franco. She decided Isandro wouldn't waste time on idle flattery, whereas Franco was a smooth-talker. She wondered for a moment why she spent too much time thinking about Isandro. She was only helping him in a family emergency.

Anna helped him prepare the meal and they talked generalities about the village and people he knew locally. Afterwards, they played cards with the children until their bedtime. Ina and Eduardo came back in their pyjamas to say goodnight, and then disappeared down the circular staircase again. Anna presumed that the evening with him had ended for her too, but he picked up their wine glasses and went out to the terrace. Anna followed him. For some reason she was glad to spend more time with him.

The waves breaking on the rocks below was the only sound. The black and rust-coloured rock edging the terrace on all sides threw long shadows along the polished granite floor. Anna picked up her glass and stood near him.

The rough taste of the wine lingered on her tongue.

He offered the information. 'Franco's coming tomorrow, to visit Teresa. He's bringing Maria with him.'

She didn't ask who Maria was. He clearly assumed she knew. Anna nodded and felt a twinge of disappointment.

'Perhaps we can go out together for a meal? I'm sure Juanita would babysit.'

Anna found the prospect of another evening out with the Rodriguez clan was not so pleasing this time, and wondered why. She liked Franco and her opinion of Isandro had improved in leaps and bounds too. She didn't usually mind meeting new people.

She quipped, 'Franco may already have other arrangements. I bet he has dozens of local girlfriends, doesn't he? I expect it's hard for him to keep up with them all sometimes.' Without thinking, she added, 'He's a very accomplished flirt, isn't he?'

Isandro laughed and nodded. His eyes glittered in the darkness. 'Franco uses every God-given opportunity to go out with attractive women, as long as there are no strings attached. What he needs is to fall for someone who calls his bluff.'

She chuckled. 'He will one day, I'm sure. He's a nice person and a very lovable flirt.'

'Do you have someone special waiting at home?'

She fondled her glass and looked at the reflection of the moon, bobbing like a silver globe on the waves. 'No. I've several good friends, male and female, but no unique boyfriend. I haven't found a special love. Perhaps I'm hoping for too much but I don't want insincerity from some man, any man, just to fill the gaps in my life. I don't want to mess up someone else's life, and I don't want someone to walk slipshod over my life either.'

He stared out across the dark water. 'So you lock yourself up in an ivory tower after work?'

Impatiently, she retorted, 'Of course

not. I just don't intend to pretend, or agree to loose relationships that focus only on sex. I'll either meet someone special one day, or not. I'd rather stay single than end up living with someone only because I'm afraid to be on my own and lonely.'

He leaned against the balustrade, facing her. He cradled his glass in his hands and looked at her. He questioned, 'You've never had a lasting relationship?' She could see his eyes glisten despite the shadows.

She concentrated on her words. They wedged in her throat for a moment. 'Yes, once — a long time ago at university. It turned out to be a disaster because Phillip got bored with our relationship but didn't tell me. I don't know why he just didn't admit it was over but he didn't. I was gullible and stupid. I found out later he'd been cheating on me with friends and complete strangers for a long time. It's probably why I don't trust anyone easily anymore.' She laughed softly.

'Anyway, at the moment I'm very glad a steady relationship isn't complicating my life. I'm facing a serious decision.'

'What about?' He sipped his wine.

'My brother went to live in Australia four years ago. My parents are visiting him at present and they love it. When my dad retires in a couple of years, they're thinking of moving permanently. They want me to join the rest of the family.'

'You mean settle there?' He whistled softly. 'That's quite a step. And . . . have you decided?'

She shook her head. 'No. I love my parents and I'd do anything for them, but I don't need them anymore.' She paused. 'Do you understand what I mean?' He nodded. 'It's lovely being with them, visiting them, sharing all kinds of memories, and if they go, I'll miss them like crazy but I don't want to give up everything that makes me happy here, to start looking for exactly the same down under.'

'Then don't do it! Australia is far away, but a non-stop flight will get you there in twenty-four hours and there's always Skype and emails. They may return again sooner than anyone imagines, once the initial fascination wears off. That happens to an awful lot of people. They miss their neighbours, or the local pub, or their garden.'

Talking to him helped. 'Yes, I think you're right. That could happen. They have a lovely garden and spent years planning and caring for it. Gardening is one of their main hobbies.'

'Incoming pensioners don't face residency restrictions, if they can support themselves.'

'It sounds like you know about the pros and cons?'

'I visited Australia for a while when I was at university. I loved the easy-going atmosphere but I'm happier in Europe. My work functions better here.'

'My parents would never force me to do anything.'

'Then just follow your instincts.'

Anna changed the subject. 'Franco said your girlfriend is a TV presenter?'

He took a sip of the wine. 'Yes. Maria is clever. She knows what she wants and how to get it.'

'So do you!' He gave a low chuckle and something inside her tingled. 'Franco is a lovable flirt, and you're more serious about everything. Do you believe in love?'

He shrugged. 'Life these days is fast, furious, and feelings are often shallow ones, aren't they? Passion is given and taken without any kind of long-term planning behind it. I'm not sure if I believe in love, or not. Or whether I want to be bound, or not. You seem to want permanency and love ever after. I'm not sure that it exists.'

She took a liberal sip of the heady wine. 'From your girlfriend's viewpoint, that's not a very flattering remark, is it? Do you realize you have the same attitude as Franco? Whereas he candidly flirts with loose intentions, you are honest and direct, but also avoiding commitment, aren't you?'

He looked unruffled. 'Maria knows how I feel and she doesn't want to be chained either.'

'Chained? What a strange description. Wanting to belong to someone doesn't chain you, does it? If you feel chained, something's wrong. You can love someone and still be free. Men are more sex-orientated than women are, and I think women still look for romantic love, but sex won't keep a relationship alive for ever. Commitment, tolerance and sex go hand in hand.' He lifted his brows but didn't comment. Anna continued. 'People like my parents and yours have stayed together because they've learned to accept the other person's faults, and because they love and respect them. It would be wonderful if I met someone who accepts my shortcomings and still loves me for what I am. Short-lived physical attraction is a one-way street.' She paused. 'Sorry! I'm not intending to be personal. It's none of my business what you or anyone else thinks, or does. This wine must be very heady. After a couple of glasses, I'm starting to sound maudlin. Perhaps I'm drunk. Don't take any notice. I'm simply old-fashioned.'

She felt embarrassed. He probably thought her completely out of touch with today's world.

He sat down on the edge of the balustrade, rested his arms on his thighs and cradled his glass. With a ghost of a smile, he said, 'But very likeable. There's nothing wrong with believing that you're right and other people are wrong, He reached out for her glass. 'Let me get you some more wine.'

7

Franco phoned and persuaded her to come on the 'foursome'. He told her Isandro had already organised his housekeeper to stand guard over the children for a few hours.

* * *

She decided to wear a simple black linen dress. The sun had bleached her blonde hair a tone lighter and Anna decided someone would pay a lot of money in a London saloon for the same effect. She considered her face in the mirror and added some oriental-looking earrings. They looked good and they boosted her self-confidence. She was curious to see what kind of woman Isandro liked. The other three picked Anna up at the hotel. Apart from exchanging polite greetings, Anna and

Maria didn't talk on the drive to the restaurant. Nobody noticed because Franco kept up a constant flow of chitchat and conversation.

Waiting for the waitress to show them to their table, Anna at last had time to study Isandro's girlfriend. She noticed that Maria was studying her in return.

She was tall, almost on eye-level with Isandro. She had flashing, almond-shaped black eyes, and a smooth olive complexion. The beautifully cut, thick black hair flowed around her shoulders. She had a thin nose, classically high cheekbones, and very attractive features. Anna could understand why she was a popular presenter. Her looks gave her a head start over any other competitors. Even though her smile didn't reach her eyes, she managed to conceal her lack of interest very well. She had a slim, shapely figure and knew how to use make-up to her best advantage. She looked like a model with bored eyes. Anna told herself not to be so critical. She tried to be pleasant. Maria didn't reciprocate so, after a while, Anna gave up trying. Despite that, it turned out to be an enjoyable evening. Franco kept a lively repartee flowing back and forth, so the men were unaware that the two women weren't on the same wavelength. Anna watched Isandro and Maria out of the corner of her eye and how Maria touched his arm possessively with her red-tipped fingers. Now and then, she ran them down his arm seductively and looked at him with hidden suggestions in her eyes. For some unknown reason the gesture annoyed Anna. Isandro was polite and attentive but there was something missing. No passion, no visible pleasure that they were spending time together. Anna reminded herself it was none of her business. The food turned out to be very good.

A local guitarist played some music. Anna's eyes sparkled when she clapped in rhythm along with other tourists. The two men eyed their British guest indulgently but Maria looked bored to tears. Anna was still glad she'd met the Rodriguez family. They'd made an ordinary holiday seem special.

Some hours later, Isandro left his jeep standing and they all strolled back through the cobbled streets. When they reached the turn-off to Anna's hotel, Franco quickly offered his company as far as the entrance, but Anna insisted he carry straight on with the others.

Maria laughed. 'Has Anna ruined your plans for this evening Franco?'

He answered, tongue in cheek, 'How did you guess?'

Anna laughed softly, before she said her goodbyes to everyone. Leaving Franco still flirting outrageously with her, she walked down the narrow alleyway and didn't look back.

★   ★   ★

When she got ready for bed, she mused that Maria would be in bed with Isandro by now. She didn't want to think about them together. Maria wasn't right for him, but she couldn't define why. They were both unusual personalities, but a good relationship needed something more than that to make it work. Maria was too egoistic and career-orientated. She only came to life if someone asked her about her job. Anna didn't want to imagine them together or making love. It took her a long time to fall asleep.

★ ★ ★

Two days later in her room, she picked up the phone.

'Hello!'

'Anna, Isandro here. Sorry to bother you again, but I don't know who else I can ask at such short notice. I've got to go to Barcelona tomorrow morning to answer technical queries about my plans. I only just found out they want to talk to me, otherwise I'd have tried to put them off until next week or at least until I could organize help. Juanita, my cleaner, is in bed with some kind of virus.'

'And you'd like me to look after the children?'

'Yes. Teresa will be back from hospital the day after tomorrow, but I need help now. If you've something special arranged for this evening or tomorrow morning, please just say so. I might be able to leave the kids in the waiting room when I'm in Barcelona, but prospective clients don't like you bringing personal problems along when professional discussions are in progress.'

Anna laughed. 'I can imagine. It's no problem. What time would you like me to come?'

'Would you mind staying overnight with them until I come back sometime late tomorrow morning or early afternoon?'

'No, that's okay. I presume that means you'd like to leave sometime this afternoon?'

'If possible! It would give me time to

ask about which aspect they want to discuss tomorrow, before the office closes today.'

'I'll be glad to help, as long as the children don't mind.'

'They like you. They keep telling me that Anna never interferes like I do.'

She chuckled. 'That's children.'

'I'm taking them to see Teresa now. We'll be back before four.'

'Then I'll come at four-thirty.'

★   ★   ★

She rang the bell and Eduardo and Ina came tearing down the corridor; Anna could see them through the smoked glass inset before they reached her. They opened the door and gave her a welcoming smile.

Ina asked, 'Can we play cards this evening?'

Eduardo added, 'And swim before we go to bed.'

Anna laughed. 'We'll see. Can I come in first?'

They let her pass. Isandro came towards her. Her heartbeat intensified and she reminded herself not to be silly.

'Come in.' He reached for her bag. Anna let go when their fingers touched. Following him down the corridor, she asked, 'How's Teresa?'

'She's very well. She wanted to leave the clinic days ago, but we persuaded her to stay. She and the children will go back home with my parents, when they come to pick them up at the weekend.' He gestured her towards the roomy white couch. She sat down obediently and the children stood nearby watching and listening.

'That's a good idea. When do Eduardo and Ina go back to school?'

'No idea, that's not my responsibility.'

The children chimed in, 'Not for ages yet.'

Isandro smiled and Anna took a deep breath while watching him.

'My mother will help keep an eye on them when they're with my parents. It gives Teresa a breathing space. I'm working and visiting sites all the time. Teresa knows she's always welcome, but she'll be better off if she stays with my parents for a while.'

Anna nodded. 'I expect so.'

'Would you like something to drink?'

'No, I'm not thirsty. Don't worry about me. The children will help to find anything I need. What do I make them for supper?'

'Whatever you like. Have a look in the fridge or the storeroom.' He looked at the metal surface of his watch. 'If you don't mind, I'd like to get away.'

Anna nodded. 'Of course.' She studied him. He stood nonchalantly with his hands in the pockets of his trousers. Dressed casually in a white shirt and beige chinos, his aftershave smelt of pine and the countryside, a pleasant fragrance that emphasised his personality.

He stared at her a little longer than necessary and then said, 'Are you sure? I'm very grateful. We seem to be taking advantage of you all the time. Considering how I ordered you off my property the first time we met, you're being extremely supportive. I don't know how to repay you.'

She gestured with her hand. 'It's perfectly okay. If I didn't want to help, I'd say so. I can be decisive and determined when necessary.'

He tilted his head to the side. 'Really? You seem to be an extraordinarily well-balanced and friendly person.'

'You haven't seen me controlling a classroom of twenty-five children who are determined to make Monday morning unbearable!'

Ina came across. 'Come to see your room. We bought flowers for Mama this morning and an extra bunch for you. I put them in a vase on your bedside table.' She took Anna's hand.

'That's very kind. I'd love to see them.'

Isandro said, 'I'll be off then.' He handed her a piece of paper. 'My mobile number.'

Anna took it and nodded. 'We'll be fine.'

Isandro gave her a searching look, and nodded. He picked up his attache case and some rolled blueprints. He was ready to go. She followed Ina down the circular stairs leading to the lower level.

* * *

They had fun playing a never-ending card game. The children wanted to swim afterwards, so Anna borrowed one of Teresa's swimsuits and secretly relished the chance to enjoy the luxury of his pool. The deluxe feeling of the warm water flowing across her body and the sun gradually slipping away behind the horizon, made the moment unique. Floating on her back in the turquoise water, she lifted her head to look out over the endless sea. Sheer perfection! It also solved the problem of whether she should insist on the children having a shower before they went to bed.

★ ★ ★

They agreed on baguette sandwiches for supper. Anna didn't mind cooking and quite enjoyed it whenever time allowed, but she wondered if Spanish children had other tastes. She found some baguette bread wrapped in a clean teacloth in the kitchen. Looking fresh and clean after their swim, Anna watched them munch their way through a couple of pieces of baguette with ham and cheese. They drank cocoa while Anna helped herself to a baguette sandwich. It tasted wonderful. The sun flamed on the horizon and they watched it as they ate. It gradually slid behind the horizon leaving a crimson sky that painted the heavens in breath-taking colour for a while longer.

She looked back at the house. The lines reminded Anna slightly of a modern museum. She loved the figurative and almost abstract look of it all. She admired the way Isandro had incorporated the natural rock into the building. Some of the house's inside walls were just bare rock. He'd solved the use of the available space to perfection in every room, on every level. Black and white furnishings and touches of stainless steel gave the rooms an aesthetic appearance, and the sense of simplicity made everything just right. Most of all Anna loved the wonderful views, because all the main rooms looked out to sea. Only the entrance hall and the guest toilet faced the courtyard or the road beyond. What she saw confirmed her initial impression the first time she saw it the house was very special and quite perfect.

The children made lots of excuses to linger. Anna let them. They told her about their last school, about their current friends, and how they'd like to have special friends one day. Moving around constantly might give them a cosmopolitan background, but it didn't help when you were ten years old and wanted a permanent friend to play with at the end of the day. Eventually, they couldn't pretend any longer. They yawned non-stop. Anna went down below with them, waited while they cleaned their teeth and then she tucked them into bed. She allowed them to read for a while and guessed that sleep would soon overtake them.

Upstairs she helped herself to a glass of wine and went out onto the terrace. The wind felt soft and balmy on her skin, and she sat on the edge of a terrace step with her arms wrapped around her knees like a leprechaun. She simply enjoyed being there at that moment. The sky now flaunted an enormous silver moon and a brilliant collection of twinkling stars.

* * *

Finally, she went inside and closed the doors. Eduardo had proudly shown her how to lock up, before he went to bed. She checked the doors and windows, and put out the lights. Anna looked in on the children on her way to her room.

It was next door to theirs. They were fast asleep and their books lay neglected. She got ready for the night in the small, flawless en-suite bathroom. Propping herself up with an extra pillow, she drifted for a while into the plot of her latest read. Soon her lashes kept brushing her cheeks and she had to jog her concentration. She gave up, put the book aside and put out the light.

8

Something interrupted her sleep. Dazed, she reached out and fumbled for the light. Something was moving upstairs. She listened. There it was — the same sound again! She sensed it wasn't Isandro. He would have warned her, by phone, if he intended to return early.

She felt sure someone unwanted was upstairs. With a pounding heart, she put out the light, went to the door and opened it silently. Only the sparse lighting from a large window at the end of the corridor helped her to see anything. Hushed movements and flashes of light filtered through the darkness. She thought briefly about going back to her room, locking the door and stuffing the pillow over her ears. She didn't. She had to protect the children and was responsible for the house. If she confronted whoever it was, there might be a chance they'd scuttle off without causing any trouble.

She tiptoed barefoot up the circular stairway and tried to remember the location of the light switches. The moonlight shone through the floor-length windows and a shadowy figure was lifting something off the wall. The sketch! Isandro's Picasso! Driven by sheer anger, she forgot about caution and dashed for the light switch. Next to the wall stood a big man dressed in dark colours and with a woollen mask pulled over his face. Anna could only see the dark glitter of his black eyes through the slits of his mask. Her unexpected appearance clearly shocked him.

Taken unaware, he swore under his breath. Barely hesitating, he began to stuff the framed sketch into a roomy sack. Anna hurled herself at him and tried to seize the sack. She presented him with no real challenge. He pushed her roughly aside and Anna fell onto the floor next to the leather sofa. The noise attracted someone else from the next room. A second man, slightly shorter in stature, took in the situation at a glance. He bellowed at the other one in Spanish. Ignoring Anna, they both rushed towards the entrance.

Unhurt, Anna still felt shocked. Struggling to her feet, she ran after them. By the time she caught up, they were already outside. In their hurry, they'd left the door open. A dilapidated delivery van stood in the small court-yard. One of them wrenched the driver's door open and clambered in. The second one, carrying the sack, ran around to the passenger seat and pulled at his mask. Without it, Anna saw his face for a couple of seconds and he looked at her with a nasty expression. The engine howled to life; he sprang inside. The van reversed up the short driveway out onto the road. With its wheels screeching, it sped off in the direction of the coastal road to Barcelona.

★ ★ ★

Anna slid down the doorframe and stared unbelieving into the darkness. Damn it! She'd concentrated on the man's face after he removed his mask. She'd forgotten to note the car's registration number. Struggling to her feet, she noticed how her hands trembled. She locked the door behind her. Checking quickly, the furniture and fittings looked undamaged. She couldn't imagine how they'd got in. She went down to check on the children, but they were still fast asleep. She noticed her legs were shaking. In the living room, she looked at her watch. It was four a.m.. Should she phone Isandro, or the police? She opted for Isandro. She didn't like disturbing him, but it was his house and if she phoned the local police, they might not understand her because of language difficulties.

Grabbing the paper with his mobile number from where she'd left it in the kitchen, she punched it in and waited. It rang several times before a sleepy-sounding Isandro said, 'Si, Rodriguez!'

'Isandro? This is Anna. I'm sorry to disturb you, but someone has broken in. They've stolen your Picasso drawing and perhaps other items too.'

Wide-awake now, he sounded shocked. 'What! Are you okay? What about the children?'

'We're fine. I woke up when I heard them moving around upstairs. I disturbed them, and they left in a hurry. I don't know if I should contact the police. What would you like me to do? I might get someone on the phone who doesn't understand English properly.'

He sounded like he was still absorbing the news. 'You should have locked yourself in with the children. Burglars wouldn't waste time to break down a locked door.'

'When I heard them, I thought it might be you returning for something, but decided you would have warned me you were coming. I soon realized they were burglars when I saw one in the process of pinching your Picasso. They panicked and made a quick exit in a van going in the direction of Barcelona.

'You took a risk. Are you sure that you're okay?'

Impatiently she said, 'Yes, I'm fine. What do you want me to do?'

He paused. 'I'll phone the police here and ask them. Pour yourself a stiff drink. I'll call you back as soon as possible. Thank heavens they didn't turn violent.'

'Okay. Sorry to mess up your sleep.'

He snorted audibly. 'As if that matters!'

Anna made herself a cup of coffee and added a dash of cognac. Her mind still circled wildly. A short time later, he phoned back.

'The police here will contact the local ones. They'll probably be with you soon. I warned them that you don't speak Spanish. I could come back.'

'What for? You might lose the commission if you do. You weren't here when it happened, so you can only tell them what's missing.'

He sounded determined. 'I could

drive back straight away and still be here in time for the meeting.'

Impatiently, she said. 'Don't be silly. Finish your business in Barcelona; that's your first priority. I'll tell the police that you'll contact them on your return. It won't make any difference if they get a list of stolen items half a day later, and you can't do more than that right now.

To her surprise, he was silent for a moment.

'I don't like you facing this all on your own, but you clearly don't need me.'

She laughed. 'I'll keep you in the picture, promise.'

★　★　★

The police arrived at *Casa Grande* a short time later. One young policeman spoke very good English, so there was no difficulty when she explained what had happened. She tried to describe the man's face. They checked for finger-prints and found nothing. The burglars had forced the small window in the toilet. By the time the police left, the children were already awake. Dawn shone brightly with the promise of another sunny day ahead.

* * *

The children felt they'd missed all the fun and were disappointed. Feeling tired and drained, Anna got them breakfast. She already knew that Spaniards never had much for breakfast. The children wanted orange juice and slices of buttered bread with jam. She was glad when they stated they'd like to play on the terrace. The sunshine grew hotter. They romped in the pool, played with their Nintendo, and drew some more pictures for Teresa. Anna was too nervous to fall asleep but it helped to lean back and let the sun cover her body.

* * *

Isandro arrived after lunch, and Anna's heart sank when she saw Maria was with him. She smiled stiffly and hoped she looked welcoming.

After greeting the children, he turned to her. 'Sure you're okay?' He immediately noticed a bruise on her arm, and touched it lightly. His fingertips on her skin stirred something inside. 'I thought you said nothing happened?'

'Oh, that. It's nothing. I fell against the couch when one of them pushed me.'

'Heaven forbid! They could have got really nasty.'

Anna noticed how Maria eyed them carefully.

'Perhaps, but they didn't.' She picked up a card from the nearby table. 'The police gave me this. They want you to give them a list of what's missing with descriptions or photos.'

He took the card, shoved it into the breast pocket of his pale blue shirt, and nodded. Looking at him, something unexpected churned her insides

103

around. The burglary must have shaken her up more than she knew. She had a lump in her throat, and the feeling that her mind wasn't functioning properly anymore. She got to her feet quickly.

Maria said sharply in English, 'Check carefully what's disappeared since you left yesterday, Isandro. Opportunity makes all kinds of thieves.' She eyed Anna spitefully.

For a moment, Anna didn't react; then she paled under her tan. 'I hope you're not suggesting I pinched something, or that I invented the burglary? What a ridiculous idea! Why should I?'

Maria fingered a fold in her silk blouse and fussed with her white trousers. 'In my job you hear the strangest stories sometimes.'

Isandro turned towards her and looked angry. 'Don't be stupid. That's a very brainless and hurtful remark.'

Maria moved closer and slung her arm around his neck. He freed himself quickly. His reaction rattled Maria and she hurried to justify herself. 'You're too trusting, Isandro. I just meant that these days, anything is possible.'

Anna glared at Maria, wanted to explode, but managed to curb her temper. There must be something special about Maria that attracted him, although she couldn't imagine what. She wouldn't argue with her or cause trouble between them; she just wanted to steer clear of Maria and her poisonous tongue. 'I assure you I've never stolen anything from anyone, in my whole life.'

Maria shrugged but didn't comment.

Anna had to get away. She looked at Isandro. 'I'll fetch my things. You know where I am if the police want to contact me.' The children stood watching them all and Anna smiled at them. 'We'll see one another soon, I expect.'

His mouth tightened. 'I hope you're not paying any attention to Maria's stupid remarks. Don't rush off. At least have coffee with us. Tell me again what happened exactly, and what the police said. Maria spends too much time in the world of sensational news items. She's always expecting to find a dramatic situation, even when there's not a hint of anything on the horizon. I'm certain you had nothing to do with the burglary. I'm very grateful that you stayed and took care of the children. I know my cleaning lady would have panicked. You coped marvellously.'

Annoyed, Maria's eyes blazed. 'You don't need to apologise on my behalf, Isandro. I made a perfectly sensible remark. If Anna thought it sounded like an accusation that's her problem not mine.'

Anna didn't want to listen anymore. She hurried downstairs, her shoes clattering as she dashed to her room. She threw her clothes haphazardly into her small holdall. When she returned to the living room, Maria had disappeared. Isandro stood staring of the window with his hands thrust in his pockets. He turned when he heard her.

'Please, don't rush away. I can understand why she's upset you, but ignore her. I trust you completely.'

She nodded. 'I hope so, but it isn't a good idea for me to stay anymore.' She paused. 'Have you noticed if anything else is missing, apart from the sketch?'

'I haven't checked everything but I noticed there are a couple of small sculptures missing from the hall. Nothing very valuable.'

'Perhaps you'll be lucky and get them back. I wonder why those men knew you had something worth stealing.'

He shrugged. 'They probably had their eyes on exclusive-looking houses and checked in advance by looking or asking about the contents. I expect they thought no one was here when they saw the empty courtyard.' When he noticed Anna hitching her bag to her shoulder, he said, 'If I can't persuade you to stay, let me drive you back to the hotel.'

She picked up the holdall. 'No need, really. It's downhill all the way.'

Maria marched into the living room in a flowing beach robe and adjusted her large sunglasses on her nose. She paused to consider them and gave Anna a haughty glance before she moved on. Passing Isandro, she said, 'Get me a drink, darling will you?'

* * *

Anna went towards the door without another word. Outside she plonked her sunhat on her head and, with her eyes glistening with angry tears, she set off.

She didn't generally brood over negative situations because she'd learned you couldn't change the past. It was better to move on and forget it. She knew he wouldn't have left her with the children in the first place if he doubted her honesty. Maria was spiteful, not Isandro.

She still felt downhearted and miserable. Why had Maria acted so nastily? She was attractive, a renowned TV personality, and she was Isandro's girlfriend. What more did she want?

9

When she reached the hotel, she found Señora Mendora watering the geraniums in the terracotta pots either side of the doorway.

'Ah, our English visitor! Is Señor Rodriguez back? Is everything all right? Any difficulty with the children?'

'He's back, and the children were good, but there was trouble.'

Señora Mendora looked puzzled. 'Trouble? What trouble? She waited expectantly.

Anna explained and gave her a summary of the previous night's happenings.

The older woman's worn hand flew to her mouth and her kind eyes widened. 'And you all alone with those two children. *Madre de Dios*! Even if some of us were sceptical about Señor Rodriguez in the beginning, now we know him better, we like him. He shops in the village and isn't one of those jet-set characters you read about in the newspaper. He's friendly but keeps himself to himself and that's how we like it. He joins in our local celebrations, and is involved in our local politics. Did those evil men hurt you?'

Anna shook her head. 'No. I think they didn't expect to find anyone in the house, and panicked when they saw me.'

'Thank heavens you weren't hurt. Leave your bag by the counter. I'll make us coffee and you can tell me all about it.'

Anna repeated her story. Señora Mendora's comments calmed her and helped to put things back into perspective again.

* * *

She felt tired and went upstairs to sleep. A brisk walk around the town later that afternoon, a little shopping for her personal needs in the shops near the harbour, and a meal in the courtyard that evening filled up the rest of the day, before she settled down for the night with a book and tried not to think about Isandro or the *Casa Grande* anymore.

★ ★ ★

Next morning after breakfast, she drove off with no particular goal in mind and ended up in a small village that had little to recommend it except for an old marketplace. She sketched a little with the sun blazing down. Checking the map, she noticed she'd almost gone full circle again. On the way back to the village, she appreciated the air-conditioning in the car. Negotiating her way carefully through the busy streets, she parked on the slope behind the hotel. She felt hot and untidy and decided to go down to the beach for a swim. Scarcely in the lobby again, Señora Mendora came bustling out of the back room.

'Someone phoned when you were out.'

Anna's heart accelerated. 'Who?'

'Teresa de Arroyo.'

Her pulse steadied. She'd forgotten that Teresa was leaving hospital today.

'She wants you to phone her back.'

Anna nodded. 'I will. Do you have the number, Señora?'

Señora Mendora went behind the desk and ruffled through books looking for the telephone directory. She flipped through the pages with the tips of her fingers, reached for a piece of paper, wrote the number down, and handed it to Anna.

'Thanks! I'll phone from my room.'

She took the steps two at a time. Dumping her bag, she opened the bedroom window and reached for the telephone. Punching in the number, she absent-mindedly shoved the paper into her bag and hung it over the bedpost while listening to the phone ringing.

'Hullo.'

Anna recognised Teresa's voice. 'Teresa,

it's Anna. How super to hear your voice. How are you feeling?'

'I'm fine, although the way that Isandro fussed you'd think I have a bleeding six-inch slash across my stomach.'

Anna laughed. 'Men are helpless when someone is ill, aren't they? My father falls apart if my mum only has a cold. I'm glad you're okay again. Isandro said you're going to stay with your parents for a while?'

'Yes, that's why I phoned. I want you to come up before I go. I want the chance to thank you for your help.'

'That's not necessary. The children were fantastic, and Isandro cared for them nearly all of the time.'

'I know all that, but no one could expect a stranger to give up their holiday to help in the way you did. You were great. Anyway, I'm bored, and I want to hear all about the break-in too. How awful for you; it must have been frightening. I promised Isandro not to leave the house until my parents arrive sometime tomorrow, so I'd love some company.'

Anna paused. 'I'd like to see you, of course, but I don't want to intrude on Isandro and Maria.' She paused but then decided it didn't matter if she said what she thought. 'She doesn't like me much.'

Teresa answered honestly. 'Maria doesn't like any other woman — full stop! That's the main reason why I've agreed to go to my parents'. I've stayed with Isandro for a couple of weeks already. I'm sure Isandro doesn't mind but Maria can be bitchy. I don't know what he sees in her, apart from her looks. I notice there's more tension in the air these days too. I'm not certain if the children and I are the cause of her touchiness, or if she's always so difficult. I do know that Maria was in a tizzy about something this morning. She went tearing off back to Barcelona straight after Isandro brought me back from the hospital. She could barely manage a polite goodbye. I'm not sure if she chose to go, or if they'd had some kind of tiff.' Sounding almost cheerful, she continued. 'If they did quarrel, and she expected Isandro to go after her, she'll be disappointed.'

Anna didn't comment.

Teresa shouted to the children. Anna heard them splashing in the pool in the background. 'Isandro isn't here. He's visiting a client further down the coast, someone who wants him to design a house perched half-way up a mountain in the middle of nowhere.'

That meant she wouldn't have to face Isandro. Anna still felt awkward about yesterday. She also wished the burglary hadn't happened during her stay. Isandro was the source of too many questions in her mind; one question followed the next, and she didn't want to start dreaming about something that could never happen.

'I intended to go to the beach this afternoon but I'll come up and visit you instead.'

'Bring your gear with you; you can

swim in the pool. The children tell me all about how you kept them busy with something new and interesting all the time.'

Anna laughed softly. 'That's the teacher in me.'

Teresa said, 'Well you must be a good teacher because the children like you. I'm going to mix us all some cold drinks, so wing your way up here as fast as you can.'

★ ★ ★

They spent a pleasant afternoon together. The sun blazed down out of a cloudless blue sky. Anna had gained a lovely honey-coloured tan, but she still continued to plaster herself with sun cream. Apart from swimming in the pool now and then, she spent the time with Teresa on loungers, under a huge sunshade. They chatted, and Anna could tell that Teresa's stay in hospital had now increased her fears about leaving her children behind.

'If I'm not around now, when will I

be? When they're a few years older they'll automatically drift away from us, but at the moment we need to be there.'

'Some boarding schools are very good, but I can understand how you feel. They're great kids. Work it out with your husband.'

'Um! He'll be back soon and we must find a solution to suits us all.'

When the sun reached its zenith, Anna looked at her watch. She wanted to leave before Isandro arrived. 'I'm off.' She got up and slipped into a loose sundress. 'I enjoyed our chat and loved seeing you and the children again. Take care of yourself Teresa, and of your family.'

'We'll keep in touch, I hope? Perhaps we'll meet again one day.'

'Perhaps, who knows?' Anna didn't think it very likely.

'Give me your telephone number or your email address. If you like, I'll let you know how we are and what we're doing.'

Anna ruffled through her bag and

gave her a visiting card. 'It's all on there. I'd love to hear from you.'

She hugged the two children. She honestly liked them and they smiled back confidently.

'Send me a card or an email one day, Ina. I promise to reply.'

Ina nodded.

Eduardo added defiantly. 'I'll send you one too.'

Teresa went with her to the door. Anna gave her a hug. They were on the brink of parting when Isandro's jeep drove into the courtyard. He jumped out and viewed them both speculatively. Anna's eyes froze on his long, lean form and felt her colour heighten and her knees became jelly. She hoped no one noticed. Why did he have such a stupid effect on her?

Teresa said, 'Anna's off. She's been here all afternoon, keeping me company.'

Isandro nodded and said casually, 'Stay for a meal and a drink?'

Anna hurried to reply. 'Thanks, that's

very kind, but I've something planned already.'

His white teeth contrasted pleasingly with his olive skin when he smiled and said, 'Want a lift back to the hotel?'

Anna resisted and shook her head.

He didn't persist, and Anna gave Teresa a parting kiss on her cheek. She gave him a parting smile and set off. When she reached the road, they were all still standing in the doorway. She lifted her hand and hurried away.

* * *

When Teresa cleared up after the children, she found Anna's sunglasses. Isandro viewed them with interest and held out his hand.

'I'm going to get some wine for dinner. I'll hand them over.'

Teresa wondered why he needed to buy more wine when his storeroom was already stacked from the floor to the ceiling, but she didn't comment.

In the village, he parked on the main street and set out for Anna's hotel clutching her glasses. Rounding the corner, he spotted Anna. She was busy, hugging a man with blond hair and blue eyes. She smiled when she looked up into his face. Isandro guessed he must be a fellow countryman. They began to laugh. Isandro stopped in his tracks and pivoted quickly before she noticed him. He deliberated for a moment and then stuffed the glasses into his pocket. He couldn't hurry straight back and face Teresa's questions yet. He detoured to the village store where he bought a couple of bottles of wine. When he passed the Mendoras' hotel again, he saw no one. Anna was entitled to meet whomever she liked. He walked inside briskly. Señora Mendora came bustling when he rang the bell. 'Miss Coleman forgot these when she visited my sister this afternoon. Is she here?'

'Yes, I think so. An old friend turned up unexpectedly just now and I think they're going out for a meal together. She said he's a fellow teacher. It's nice for her to have a visitor from home.'

A muscle moved in his jaw. 'Yes, I expect so.'

'Heard anything from the police about the burglary, Señor?'

'No, not so far.' Isandro guessed she hoped for news to fill the village grapevine.

She clucked sympathetically. 'Anna told me all about it. Don't give up hope. Perhaps the police will catch them.'

He nodded. At that moment, Anna came down the stairs with someone in her wake. When she saw him, she hesitated and the man behind her almost collided with her.

Isandro explained why he was there, and handed her the glasses.

'Thanks! I haven't even missed them. This is Mike, a friend of mine.'

Isandro nodded and held out his

hand. Mike took it.

'Anna told me about your burglary. Nasty that. Lucky nothing happened to her.'

'Yes, I agree.' He looked at his watch. 'I must go; my sister is waiting for the wine.'

Mike nodded. 'Nice to meet you!'

Anna added, 'We're going to that restaurant in Val Parieso, without a reservation.'

He considered her face carefully. 'It shouldn't be a problem. It's always busy in the holiday season, but you should be okay today. They are packed out on Saturdays. Enjoy yourselves. Goodbye, Mr . . . .'

'Mike.'

Isandro nodded, and with a last look at them, he left. Outside he took a deep breath and set off for home.

Mike said, 'He's a very impressive Spaniard. There's an aura about him. What does he do?'

Fussing with the straps of her shoulder bag, Anna said, 'He's an architect, a good one. Let's go in case all the tables are booked, shall we?'

* * *

Anna enjoyed Mike's unexpected visit. He was on his way to meet his girlfriend, who was staying with friends in Gerona. He'd decided to stop on the way to see if Anna was happy with his recommendation.

They were lucky„ there were some free tables and they caught up on each other's news over a delicious meal. Señora Mendora gave him a room for the night, and Anna saw him off next morning after breakfast.

10

Standing alone, she waved and smiled until Mike's car disappeared round the corner.

Anna looked thoughtful. Everyone she knew was in a serious relationship. Were other people getting more out of life than she was? Not really. She had a job she liked, a family she loved and good health. If other people were luckier in finding the love of a lifetime, she was happy for them, but there was no point in pretending she loved someone just to have a partner. She wouldn't accept anything less than lasting love, not even when she realized she'd met a man she loved, but would never have.

With every meeting, with every conversation, her love and longings for Isandro had grown. She understood now why she wanted to be with him more than anyone she'd ever met. Just being in the same room as Isandro made her pulses race in a way she'd never expected. Whenever they were together, her senses automatically heightened. She knew she shouldn't think about him but that wasn't possible. Apart from the fact he was someone else's boyfriend, he was a Spaniard, living in Spain. He'd chosen Maria and she must accept that. Even if he were free, the difficulties would be mountainous. Anyway, why would he show interest in someone like her? She went back inside the hotel to collect her hat and her sunglasses. She'd go for a long walk along the beach to clear her head.

She wasn't likely to see the Rodriguez family again. She'd said her goodbyes to the children and Teresa, and there was no reason she should meet Franco or Isandro again. Franco spent his time in Barcelona, and Maria filled up Isandro's time. Anna wished she could accept the fact that she might never see Isandro again. She couldn't.

Her feelings were was ridiculous. She only met him a couple of weeks ago, and now she was head over heels in love with the man.

★　★　★

The beach was filling up quickly this morning, but out by the waterline it was still clear. She walked away from the village and rounded the headland to the next cove. She watched as people spread their towels and organized their children. The fresh air and change of scenery was helping a little. Seeing other people distracted her thoughts. She walked on for a while, sat on some rocks and stared into the waves trying to concentrate on her family, her work, and her friends. Somehow she always ended up thinking about the times she'd been together with Isandro. She looked at her watch. She'd have to hurry back to avoid the tide cutting her off from the village at the headland. She could always walk back via the road, but the route via the beach and the sea was nicer and shorter too.

As she strolled along, Anna wondered if it might be a good idea to drive to one of the larger towns this afternoon. She could do some window shopping and buy some replacement water colors, if she found a specialist shop. She increased her pace and pushed her windblown hair out of her face.

Climbing up the steps from the beach, a familiar voice called down to her.

'Anna!'

Teresa and the children were leaning over the wall and smiling. Teresa turned to chat in Spanish to a woman at her side, obviously explaining who Anna was. Anna could see a resemblance and guessed that she was Teresa's mother. She was a little shorter than Teresa, with salt-and-pepper hair, a clear complexion, dark questioning eyes and wearing a linen two-piece costume. The children were circling around her and adding to Teresa's information. She nodded and held out her hand when Anna drew level with them.

'How do you do. Teresa and Isandro told us how you helped to look after the children. That was very kind. You are on holiday?' Her accent was stronger than that of Teresa or Isandro, and she spoke slowly, searching for the right vocabulary, but her English was good.

'Yes. This is my first visit to Spain. I was glad to help. Eduardo and Ina are well behaved so it was a pleasure. You speak such good English. The whole family does. I feel ashamed that I can't speak a word of Spanish.'

She smiled. 'I went to a convent school and the nuns were good teachers. I think my French is better than my English and I try to remember both languages. Yes, everyone in the family speaks English well, even the children. These days you hear English everywhere. I'm sure you could learn Spanish if you wanted to. Teresa told me you're a teacher.'

Feeling relaxed, Anna said, 'Yes, I

am. I think you have a talent for languages if you manage two foreign languages with such ease.'

'I think French and English are not as difficult to learn as some other European languages.'

Anna nodded. 'You're taking Teresa home with you? That's a very good idea.'

The older woman touched her daughter's arm. 'Yes, I think so too. She feels fine, but a couple of weeks with us will do her no harm.'

Teresa laughed and rolled her eyes. 'Mother!'

Señora Rodriguez looked at Anna speculatively for a moment and asked Teresa, 'Let's invite Anna to come back and have lunch with us.'

Flustered, Anna searched for words to hinder the idea. She searched too long. The children yelled, 'Yes, Gran. Super idea!'

Teresa grinned and joined in with, 'Yes. That's an excellent idea. As long as Anna isn't planning anything more important. She's on holiday and has given up a lot of her time for the Rodriguez family already.'

Anna gave in, only thinking it was a chance to see Isandro again. Among his family it would be easier to watch him without anyone noticing. She nodded. 'Thank you. I'd like that.'

★　★　★

They walked back to the house and went out on the terrace. The women hurried to set the table and arrange the food. Anna met his father and found he looked a lot like Isandro. He was a slender man with almost aristocratic features, a straight posture and kind brown eyes.

Isandro looked pleased to see her, and Franco fussed around to make sure she had a comfortable place at the table. It turned out to be an enjoyable family lunch with fresh ham, olives, crisp bread, local cheeses and ripe tomatoes. The adults drank heady wine and the children toasted everything and everyone with orange juice. The sun shone down on them and warm breezes ruffled the table runner. There was a lot of laughter and smiles and the conversation wandered back and forth between the two languages, but Anna never felt left out. The relaxed atmosphere allowed her to be happy just to be among them.

Isandro's father viewed her cautiously at first, but he soon attuned himself to the attitude of the others. His eyes twinkled over the rim of his glass as he toasted to English-Spanish relationships. Anna could watch Isandro on the opposite side of the table to her heart's content. She only hoped no one noticed the −ffect he had on her if he looked at her.

Teresa did, but she didn't comment and hoped the gods knew what they were doing.

Anna relaxed and wondered how long she could stay without overstretching the limit of their hospitality.

No one else made a move to end the meal, except the children. They disappeared to the lower regions to read and to play. The men were discussing Isandro's chances to get the museum commission. It was clear that everyone was proud of his achievements. Anna leaned back and stored the memory for darker days ahead.

The clatter of high heels preceded Maria's sudden appearance. Anna reflected that she must have a key; no one had opened the door for her. She looked as well turned out as ever in a tight-fitting summer dress, and she smiled until her glance drifted across the table and saw Anna. The shutters came down and her eyes narrowed. She offered Isandro her cheek and he duly kissed it. Maria moved on to greet the others. Anna looked away. This was undoubtedly the right moment to leave.

When Maria reached Anna's chair she looked at Anna aggressively and uttered a barrage of Spanish in a belligerent tone. Anna didn't need to understand Spanish to know that Maria was shooting poison in her direction. Everyone around the table grew silent and they looked startled and embarrassed.

Anna got up quickly. It had been a memorable meal, but she didn't want to cross swords with Maria. Maria was on home ground and could always rant in Spanish so that Anna wouldn't understand. Anna could only defend herself if someone acted as an interpreter. She had no intention of spoiling the day for the others. Maria's enmity grew with every encounter. Anna didn't understand why. Perhaps television personalities always thought someone was out to steal their partner. Anna gave up the pretense of politeness. Without looking in Maria's direction and ignoring her outburst, she held out her hand to his father.

'It was a pleasure to meet you, Señor Rodriguez. I'm planning an outing with some other visitors at the hotel this afternoon. I have to leave now, or I'll be too late.' It was a lie, but Anna hoped it sounded genuine.

He took her hand between his. 'It was a pleasure to meet you, Anna.'

His mother smiled. 'Yes. Perhaps we'll meet again?'

Anna held her breath. 'Who knows? Thank you for the lunch. It was excellent.'

Anna hugged Teresa sitting next to her. 'Take care of yourself. Keep in touch.'

Teresa kissed her on her cheek. 'Yes, I will. And thanks again for taking care of the children.'

She hurried around the table and moved towards the living-room door. She lifted her hand quickly in the direction of Isandro and Franco. 'Bye you two. I know my way out.' She ignored Maria completely and if the others noticed it no one said anything. Isandro's mouth was a thin line. Franco's expression was incredulous puzzlement.

Anna was glad to shut the front door and lean against it for a moment before she set off down the road back to the hotel.

On her way she decided it was sensible to go away somewhere for a day or two. Perhaps she should simply cut short her holiday and leave for home but she loved the countryside and the Spanish people she'd met so far. It was wrong to let Maria spoil such a memorable holiday.

She'd never seen Maria down in the village, but wouldn't be surprised if Maria came just to make a scene. Maria was spitting poison at her, without grounds. Any woman would feel upset and jealous if another woman tried to steal her boyfriend, but Anna hadn't tried to steal Isandro. The opposite was the case. Anna had kept her longings for him well hidden. The family was leaving today, or tomorrow. In all probability Maria had to return to her work in Barcelona today or tomorrow too. Perhaps Isandro would go with her.

She mused that a couple of days visiting another area would keep her out of the way. By the beginning of next week things would calm down. From then on Anna would steer clear of any kind of contact with the Rodriguez family. She'd make excuses if any other invitation came her way, and she'd finish the last weeks of her holiday as planned. She loved Isandro but it was getting harder to accept the situation. If she could put some distance between her and him, now and later, it would help.

11

She spread the map on her bed and looked for some place within comfortable travelling distance. She decided to drive along a scenic route that started not too far away. The road ran alongside through an area of lakes. The region looked sparsely populated with only one big town on route. She could stay there overnight. She guessed she needed roughly two hours to reach the scenic road, marked in green. The town half- way along the route might provide her with somewhere to stay overnight. . .f not, she still had time to return to St. Sabatien, although she'd be late getting back. Motivated, she packed an overnight bag, and told Señora Mendora where she intended to go.

Señora Mendora clucked her disapproval and her long earrings swung spiritedly. 'That's a long way for a woman to go alone, and the roads are lonely. There isn't anything special to see on the way. There's just a lot of sheep farming and open countryside on the way to the mountains. The lakes are on the other side, because they get the rain from the north when the clouds hit the mountain sides.' She added, 'It's greener there and very picturesque, and there are lots of places to stop near the lakes, but you should take your time.'

Anna nodded. 'I will, promise. It sounds lovely. I'll be back tomorrow or the day after. If I decide to stay any longer, I'll phone you. I have your number in my cell phone.'

The older woman eyed her carefully. 'I'll get you some food. It might not be easy to find something along the way.' She disappeared into the kitchen and returned with baguette sandwiches, something that looked like a bean salad in a screw-top jar, and a bag full of alfajores. Anna recognised the Spanish fruit-and-nut biscuits. They were home-made and scrumptious. She also gave her a bottle of water, a small bottle of wine, a bottle opener and some kitchen paper and plastic cutlery. She'd thought of everything.

Anna gave her a quick hug. 'That will last me the rest of today.'

The older woman beamed and the creases on her face deepened. 'You take care, and keep your car doors locked. You never know who's about these days.'

'I will, I promise.'

★　★　★

Anna drove to the nearest petrol station, filled up and set out. She enjoyed driving and felt confident that she could manage. She'd stop in Lleida and then decide whether to carry on, or not. She wanted to ban any more thoughts about Isandro or the Rodriguez family for the rest of the day.

Outside the afternoon sun was hot but the car's air-conditioning kept temperatures at a pleasant level. Once she left the less populated areas, Anna began to enjoy the feeling of liberty. She met little traffic, and the further she went, the fewer cars she met. The road began to climb steadily. She looked out across a dry landscape spotted with ancient olives and other trees that reminded her vaguely of oaks.

The closer she got to the more mountainous regions, the scrubbier the vegetation looked, but it still supported sheep. Their white coats were like speckles of snow all over the foothills and peaks.

After a while, she noticed a light-coloured van was gaining on her. Whenever she checked her rear mirror, it drew even closer until it was directly behind her. Anna was in no hurry, and presumed the driver wanted to over-take. She steered closer to the side. The van remained where it was, right behind her. Anna paid no more attention. The road continued to climb and Anna stayed in low gear. Glancing across the landscape and enjoying the view, she reminded herself she had to keep an eye on the winding road as well as the scenery.

Sometimes sheep lay on the road ahead and they only scurried off down the reinforced banking when they heard the car. She noticed a small building far off, in a dip of the land. She guessed it was a farmhouse, and wondered why anyone chose to live in such a harsh environment. There were places nearer and more civilized not far off. Anna saw a vehicle, looking like a small toy, leaving the building and bouncing along a barely visible trail as it came towards the roadway.

She mused that life must be very difficult for whoever lived there. She checked the rear mirror and saw the van seemed to be almost touching her bumper. At first she assumed the driver was overtaking after all, but then she saw his face and felt shock. He was the burglar who'd removed his mask in the courtyard of Isandro's house. He leered at her.

Panic emerged and she steered towards the verge of the road. He closed the gap and leered again at her sideways as he deliberately buffeted the side of her car with his van. The vehicle's body jerked but she kept control. She gripped the steering wheel tighter and accelerated. Anna hoped her car would be stronger and faster than the van, but it kept pace and drew closer. She was dangerously near to the verge. The tyres sped over the loose gravel grit that edged the gradual slope down to the fields. When the van battered her car again, Anna lost control for a few seconds and it began to slither sideways down the gentle slope.

The wheels spun wildly as it increased speed. It remained upright but Anna lost precious seconds before she grabbed the steering wheel again. A large boulder along the way lifted the whole bodywork and the metal screeched as the underside slid across the rough surface before it sped on and righted itself again. The car continued its zigzag route until it a group of smaller boulders finally brought the journey jarringly to an end. Even though it was all over in a matter of seconds, Anna knew it was almost a miracle that the car was still upright. One of its back wheels still spun wildly in the air above one of the boulders. Anna didn't know, but above her, the driver got out of the van to check where she was, before he tore off in the direction of the mountains throwing up a cloud of dust as he raced away from the gravelled edge.

Anna was trapped by the safety belt, and the burst airbag had probably saved her from any serious injury. She felt numb with shock, and slowly she was aware of the silence surrounding her. She fumbled automatically with the door and struggled out of the safety belt. She half fell onto her knees, grateful for a cool breeze that cleared her brain a little. It helped reduce the confusion and muddle. She wanted to stand up but her legs wouldn't let her so she just sat in a heap, feeling weak and baffled. With her head in her hands, trying to coordinate her thoughts, Anna heard a car approaching, and panic returned. She forced herself to look up and was relieved to see a battered jeep approaching from the open fields. It was the vehicle she'd seen in the distance, a few minutes ago.

* * *

When it reached her, a small, sun-beaten middle-aged man jumped out and came across. He fired questions at her in Spanish and Anna could only lift her shoulders, shake her head. She told him she didn't understand Spanish. It was the one phrase she'd learned off by heart.

He continued to talk to her and although she felt confused, she knew that he wanted to help. He placed his arms under hers and tried to pull her to her feet. Anna struggled to help, but her legs felt like jelly and her head spun badly. Somehow, with her arm around his neck and his arm around her shoulder, he managed to get her to his jeep. The world around her began to spin again. She sank into the well-worn leather seat and for the first time in her life, Anna lost consciousness.

Viewing her, the farmer ran his hands over his face. He'd drive her back carefully to the farm. His Angelica would know what to do. He'd seen how that van had deliberately pushed her car off the road. Something was seriously wrong. They ought to phone the police. He went to Anna's abandoned car, removed the keys and picked up her shoulder bag from the ground nearby. Fixing her safety belt in his jeep, he drove back to the farm with her as slowly as the bumpy terrain allowed.

Anna remained woozy as the farmer and his wife helped her into the house. They made her lie down on the couch in the living room and his wife hurried to find a pillow and a rug. Anna had a headache and things continued to twirl around. She closed her eyes. She was grateful for peace and quiet.

He took his wife into the kitchen and she bombarded him with questions.

'What happened? Where did she come from? What's her name?'

'She drove along the highway and was going towards Lleida — you know the spot, where the road curves sharply to the left. I was on my way to the gully to look for that sheep with the black face. I looked up and I saw someone deliberately trying to push her off the road. He tried it a couple of times and finally succeeded. Her car slid down the banking, hit a boulder, and righted itself at the bottom. I thought it might turn right over, but she was lucky. I don't know who she is, but she's not Spanish. I brought her bag from her car, and the keys. Perhaps there's an address or a telephone number. She's confused, but I don't think there are any physical injuries. There's no wound or any blood. I think we should call the police and ask for an ambulance at the same time."

His wife nodded in agreement. 'I'll get her some water. It will do her good to rest but she ought to see a doctor. Go back for that overnight bag; she'll need it in hospital.'

★ ★ ★

'Rodriguez!' Isandro waited.

'Do you know someone called Anna Coleman? Her passport says she's British.'

His lips tightened. 'Yes. Why do you ask?'

The woman explained and he gripped the telephone tighter.

'We found your telephone number on a piece of paper in her handbag. No name, just a number, but I decided to try it anyway. I hoped it might be someone who knows her.'

'Yes. You did the right thing.' He wandered to the window and stared out across the sea. 'How is she?'

'When my husband brought her back to the farmhouse she was confused and groggy, but I think she's a little better now. We called an ambulance anyway, because we don't know if she's seriously hurt, or not. She could have some internal injury that we can't see. She fainted once, and that worried us. I don't know where the ambulance will take her. Probably Lleida, it's the next town.'

'Will you please ask the ambulance people where she's going, and phone me when you know? Tell me again what happened.'

The farmer's wife told him and his breath hissed between narrow lips. 'I wonder what she was doing on the way to Lleida. Why did someone want to push her car off the road?'

'We don't know. Your guess is as good as mine. We've called the police. I hope they get here before the ambulance does. My husband said he couldn't see exactly who the driver was from that distance.'

Tersely, Isandro said, 'Thanks for your help. I'm glad you called me. She's a British tourist staying in our village, St. Sabatien. I've met her several times so I know her. I'll inform the people at her hotel and ask the landlady to pack a bag.'

'She told us, with the help of a dictionary, that she had an overnight bag in her car, so my husband's gone to look for it. She didn't want us to call the ambulance, but a doctor should see her.'

'You're right. As soon as you know where they're taking her, phone me again please.'

'I will. What about her car?'

'I'll sort all that out for her, later.' Sounding resolute, he went on. 'Perhaps you'd better give me your telephone number and address, just in case!

12

She couldn't express herself in Spanish, so she gave in when they kept repeating 'ambulancia'. By the time the ambulance arrived, Anna had accepted the inevitable. Apart from a splitting headache, she felt much better and she didn't feel giddy anymore, but she understood why they wanted to send her to hospital for a check-up.

The police arrived just before the ambulance left. They listened briefly to her account and she understood from their broken English and gestures that they intended to come to the hospital tomorrow for a detailed statement. One of them gave her a visiting card. She didn't bother to try to explain about the connection to the burglary at Isandro's house. That was an impossible undertaking with no one around who could interpret properly, and because of her splitting headache. She put it off until she saw them tomorrow. She'd never been in an ambulance before, but now she was bundled into a Spanish one, and driven off to a nearby hospital.

After the ambulance left, the police noted the farmer's account of what happened and they promised to send a statement for the couple to sign.

★   ★   ★

The small city hospital was modern and well equipped. They examined Anna thoroughly and the friendly doctor on duty declared in perfect English that, apart from some bruising and slight concussion, she'd been lucky. They advised her to remain overnight and have a final examination in the morning. Anna didn't really want to, but she had nowhere to stay and no car at her disposal. They put her in a single room.

A friendly nurse spoke enough English to explain that she should lie

151

down, and stay in bed if she could, and try not to move around too much for a while. Anna changed into her pyjamas and the nurse returned with medication for her headache and a sedative for the night.

★ ★ ★

A sharp knock on the door broke the silence. She was flabbergasted when Isandro came in.

She stared at him with her mouth open. Her face was already pale and the colour disappeared completely for a few seconds before pink flooded her cheeks again. Swallowing a lump in her throat, she uttered, 'Isandro! What are you doing here? How did you know where to find me?'

He wasted no time. 'The people at the sheep farm phoned me. Teresa wanted to come with me but my father is planning to leave early tomorrow morning to avoid the weekend traffic around Barcelona. I didn't know how long it would take to find you and what kind of help you might need. I told her I could manage and she should stay. She was mad, but that's nothing new. Why the devil were you travelling through such an unfrequented part of the countryside on your own?'

The tone of his voice made her edgy. 'Pardon! It is none of your business what I do. I'm a good driver and I enjoy driving. How am I supposed to know there are madmen populating Spain's secondary road system?' Her head ached, and a dozen drums banged away inside her brain. She wanted to lean back into the pillows and die.

He crossed the room quickly. She could see the anger in his eyes and his clenched hands. 'You were stupid to take such unnecessary risks. Why didn't you stay in St. Sabatien?'

Impatiently, her own anger grew. 'Because I didn't want to, that's why! I wanted to see more of Spain and this area wasn't too far to drive from St. Sabatien. I was planning to stay overnight on the way. I'm a tourist from the UK, remember? How did you know exactly where to find me?'

He retorted angrily, 'The people who found you, unearthed my telephone number from your bag. They phoned and told me what had happened and said the ambulance was taking you to Lleida.'

She tried hard to concentrate even though her head protested. 'I had your telephone number? In my bag?'

'The people at the farm didn't understand much, and they decided they should try to find someone who knew you. They found lots of English telephone numbers and addresses in your bag, but only one Spanish telephone number on a bit of paper — mine.'

She tried to concentrate and suddenly remembered. 'Oh, yes. Señora Mendora wrote it down for me. I had to phone Teresa. I must have stuffed it in my bag afterwards.'

Irritated, he brushed her words aside

and said, 'Now tell me what happened.'

She did, and tried not to make it sound too melodramatic.

His dark features hardened and his brows drew together into a straight line. 'Do you realize how lucky you are? Your car could have spun around with you inside it. It could have even burst into flames.'

Anna held his glance. 'Yes, I know.'

There was a moment of silence. 'Did you notice the car number, or any other details that might help to trace the car?'

Anna shook her head. 'Everything happened so fast. He appeared out of nowhere and followed me for a while at a distance. Then he came closer but I didn't think anything was wrong, until he was alongside and I recognized him. From then on, I panicked. I didn't think about number plates or anything else when he started to ram the side of my car; I was too busy trying to keep control.'

His voice raised an octave. 'You recognized him?'

'Yes; he was that burglar from your break-in, the one who pulled his mask off before he got into the van.'

'What?' He uttered something inaudible under his breath.

'It's mad, isn't it? But that's what happened. I presume he wanted to frighten me because he knew I'd seen his face. He's probably afraid that I can identify him. He doesn't know that I'm just a tourist and won't be around long enough to accuse him of anything.'

Isandro looked like he was about to explode. 'I can't believe it. Some petty criminal almost kills you just because you saw his face for a few moments after a burglary at my house?'

She shrugged. 'That's my theory. Perhaps he only wanted to scare me and didn't expect that I'd lose control of the car.'

'Have you told the police all this?'

'I just told them what happened on the road. If I'd told them about his connection to the burglary at your house, they might have thought I was hallucinating. It does sound mad, doesn't it?'

'Of course it's not mad if it happened. You should have made them listen to you.'

'How am I supposed to force two Spanish policemen with middling English to listen to my non-existent Spanish? It would have been the Mad Hatter's tea party.'

He sighed with exasperation. 'So they left without knowing about the burglary and this man? It was silly not to at least try to make them understand.'

Bristling, she said heatedly, 'I'm not foolish. I'm English and don't speak any Spanish. We already lost each other in the entanglements of each other's language just by trying to explain what happened this afternoon. They're coming again tomorrow, and I'll try again then. I'll pick out some fitting vocabulary from my dictionary in advance.'

He just stared at her and both of them felt angry and annoyed.

She said pointedly, 'Thanks for asking how I feel, Isandro. Apart from a splitting headache, I'm fine. I wanted to leave hospital straight away, but I don't have a car anymore and I still have to talk to the police tomorrow. The doctor suggested it would be more sensible to stay overnight anyway, so I agreed. If the doctor throws me out of this room first thing tomorrow morning, I'll have to sit in the corridor and wait for the police. I don't know where to contact them and they are expecting to find me here. I'm not looking forward to sorting out problems with the car-rental firm tomorrow either.'

He ran a hand down his face and the annoyance vanished. He gave her a wry smile and his voice sounded rough with anxiety. 'Yes, you're right. I'm sorry. I should have asked how you were straight away. Are you okay?'

Anna didn't want to provoke him any further. He'd driven all this way just because a stranger had told him she'd had an accident. She offered him a weak smile and tried to stave off another yawn.

He lifted his brows and tilted his head to the side. His soft smile developed and spread across his face. Anna managed a tremulous smile in return and decided he was a delightful man, despite his quick temper. She wondered how Maria would react when she found out he'd come to help her.

He said, 'Don't worry about the car. I'll sort that out. Do what the doctor says and stay here.' His thoughts wandered and his fists clenched. He muttered, 'I'd like to get my hands on him.'

'I tried to give the police a description. I'm certain he's the same man who burgled your house, absolutely sure.'

Isandro turned abruptly and went to look out of the window. After a second or so, he asked, 'Do you think you could draw his picture? I saw some of the sketches you made of Teresa and the children. They're very good.'

Her eyes showed her surprise. She put her hand to her mouth and yawned. 'Yes, I think so, once my head has cleared. But the police have professionals trained to do just that.'

'Perhaps, but I'm not sure if they will follow that line of investigation if they think this was just a minor incident, just a fluke. They could put it down to the lack of driving skill until they know the whole story. They have no real evidence at the moment that he did it intentionally. Even when you tell them about what happened at *Casa Grande*, it takes time to get any information from our local police. A sketch from you might help and jog them faster into further action. If they had a picture, they could check their files.'

Drowsily Anna longed to close her eyes for a few minutes. She forced herself to stay awake, because Isandro stood next to her, watching. 'Yes, okay. If you think it will help, I'll try tomorrow.' She yawned. 'Sorry, they've given me a sedative.'

He smiled. 'Go ahead! Go to sleep! I'll sit here for a while and I'll come back tomorrow.'

With her head resting on the soft pillow, the knowledge that Isandro cared enough to sit next to her for a while and wanted to come back tomorrow was very comforting. She murmured, 'You don't have to stay and I don't expect you to come back tomorrow. I'm okay. I'll manage. It is very kind of you to bother about me in the first place. It's a long way to drive, thank you for com . . . '

Isandro sat, watching her face, how her pink pyjamas followed the contours of her body. He listened to her steady breathing.

Some time later, he spoke to the nurse on duty before he left.

13

Next morning, Anna flipped through her much-thumbed small English/Spanish dictionary and her frustration grew when she found a lot of the necessary vocabulary was missing. She tried constructing a few phrases with the necessary information, in case the police didn't speak any English. She realized how difficult communication would be, if the officer in charge didn't speak good English. When Isandro arrived straight after breakfast, a weight lifted from her shoulders and Anna felt a surge of delight. She smiled broadly.

'I didn't expect you'd drive all the way back here again this morning, but I am glad to see you.'

'Good! I'm here to help in any way I can.'

'I'm beginning to get nervous because I realize how difficult it is to explain anything to the police with my non-existent Spanish.' She lifted her dictionary. 'Most words I need are not in here.'

He smiled slowly. There was colour in her face again, and she looked a lot better this morning. 'I thought the police might turn up early, so I did too.'

She eyed him carefully and said softly, 'You must have got up at the crack of dawn.'

He shrugged. 'The rest of the family will be leaving early today. I was glad to get out of the house. Teresa was already running round in circles, packing. Franco was still asleep and will probably stay there to avoid the last minute panic, but he'll leave before I return. He has another date, with another girl, in Barcelona early this evening.' He gave her a lopsided grin. 'Anyway, I think your dilemma is partly my fault. It's the least I can do.'

'What do you mean your fault?' Anna wondered why he didn't mention Maria.

'If you hadn't been on your own in the house that night, you wouldn't have seen that man's face, and he wouldn't want revenge.'

'We don't know if he planned revenge. Perhaps he just happened to be on that road and recognized me. He decided to frighten me and have a bit of fun.'

'A bit of fun?'

Anna got up from the edge of the bed. 'It doesn't matter why he did it. I just want you to know I realize I haven't any right to your time.'

'Don't be silly. Had breakfast yet?'

Her breath quickened and her cheeks were warm. 'Yes. A Spanish breakfast is very frugal, isn't it?'

He laughed. 'Other countries, other customs. It depends what you want. Some people like an elaborate selection, others are just happy with coffee and a slice of bread. I'll get something to eat later, if you're hungry, promise.'

Trying to keep her thoughts on an even keel, she said, 'There's a lot of activity in the corridors of this hospital. Is that normal? There are always strange faces around moving up and down and back and forth.'

'Yes. Ordinary people involve themselves when family or friends end up in a Spanish hospital. It helps the medical staff and it helps psychologically too. The medical staff can concentrate on their work and family and friends solve the non-medical problems.'

Anna was comfortable in lightweight linen trousers and a short-sleeved white blouse. Her feet were bare in adventure sandals.

He gave her a questioning look. 'Have you seen the doctor yet?'

'Yes. I already had another test with dozens of plugs and cables attached to my head and they said I'm okay. I still have a headache, but it's not as bad as yesterday. They told me it's perfectly normal after what happened. The nurse gave me some tablets just now. They also said I could wait for the police in here; they don't need the room at present.'

He nodded, satisfied.

They chatted. He told her about Teresa, the children, his parents and how shocked they were when he told them about what had happened. He also talked about his latest project to pass the time. Anna felt wonderfully comfortable in his company.

'Franco told me yesterday that this girl in Barcelona is the love of his life.'

Anna's eyes widened and she chuckled. 'Really? Has that happened before?'

His firm mouth curled on the edge of laughter. 'I've lost count! Although this time, he does sound more serious. He sent his best wishes.'

She nodded her thanks. 'To be honest, I can't imagine him being serious about any woman for long, but everyone meets someone special if they're lucky.'

A firm knock on the door interrupted them. Two uniformed policemen entered. After the obligatory greeting, they began to ask her questions. At first, they tried to converse in English, but as soon as they realized Isandro was Spanish they used him as an interpreter.

They filled pages of their notebooks and formulated new questions via Isandro. They looked surprised when Isandro told them about the burglary at his house and how Anna had recognised the man in the van as one of the burglars. It generated a machine-gun exchange between the two of them. Isandro turned to her.

'I explained that you're an artist and that you'll draw them a picture of the man. They are going to check with the police in St. Sabatien for information about the break-in, and find out if they've made any progress. They would like you to hand in the sketch at police headquarters as soon as possible.'

Anna nodded.

The two men thanked her politely, shook hands with Isandro, and left.

Isandro said, 'Let's find somewhere nice and comfortable for you to do your sketch.'

'Um! A park or a public garden would be great. Somewhere quiet.'

'I'll ask where we can go, and you'll need pencil and paper.'

'I'd like to say '*gracias*' to the nurses before I leave.'

He nodded and picked up her bag.

She added, 'What would I do without you?'

He gave her a strange look and held out his other hand. Maria or no Maria, she gave in to the temptation and took it. Her hand remained there causing havoc to her emotions, until they found the duty nurse.

* * *

He remembered that he had drawing materials in his car. He'd left the jeep underneath leafy trees in a nearby road.

He locked her overnight bag away and rummaged for paper and pencils. They found a quiet green area with bushes and flowering plants close to the rear of the hospital. One hushed corner offered a welcome empty bench.

She settled down and then Isandro said, 'If I stay, I can only sit and watch, so I may as well try to sort out the car-rental company. If you finish a sketch today, we can hand it in before we drive back to the village.'

Happy that he didn't intend to leave her here and drive off without her, Anna delved into her bag and handed him all the relative papers. 'I took full coverage when I hired it. I hope that also includes what happened yesterday.' Anna gave him her driving licence, her passport and a visiting card. 'You might need these too.'

He looked at the headings on the forms. 'They have a branch-office here. This place is central for this region. I'll tell them you're still in hospital at present. If they want to see you personally we may have to go back.' He looked around. 'Pity! This is an old town with some interesting history, but today is not the right moment for you to play tourist. Another time perhaps?'

She looked up gratefully and nodded, although she doubted if she'd ever come back again. 'Thanks, it will save me a lot of hassle if you can sort it out for me.'

He dismissed her gratitude with a shake of his head. 'Stop thanking me all the time, woman!' He studied her for a moment before he headed off towards the centre of the town.

Anna watched him. He looked lean, tough and determined as he walked away with fast, unhesitating steps.

★ ★ ★

She sat in the shade. It was still early and the park provided a peaceful haven to relax. She looked at a large book belonging to Isandro he'd given her to support the empty pages of paper.

Much thumbed, it contained masses of facts about world famous architects and showed some of their best-known designs. She forced herself to concentrate on her sketch. The quiet surroundings and pleasant temperature helped. Submerged in the work, she scarcely noticed how quickly time passed. The features of the man soon began to emerge. She didn't enjoy the task much, because just drawing his features scared her a little. It was important to get the details right so she struggled on. If the police used it, they might find him, and eventually return Isandro's stolen picture.

She drew, corrected, shaded, and did her best. The sun crept across the paper and came from another direction. A long shadow fell across her drawing. She looked up.

'Good heavens. Back already. What's the time?' She looked in surprise at her watch.

He stood towering about her with an indulgent smile on his face. Anna had to force herself to concentrate on the matter in hand. 'Were you able to sort it out?'

'Most of it. They need a police report confirming that you were driving, and exactly what happened. We'll ask for one when we deliver your sketch. I'm sure you can get a preliminary report, if we ask politely. Here's your driving licence and the rest. They'll pick up the car, and provide you with a replacement soon. They can't do so until the police confirm that it wasn't your fault. We can go back to them from the police station.'

Anna took the papers. 'Did I have the right coverage, or will I face an extra bill?'

'Apparently you're okay, even if the car is a write-off.'

With relief, she said, 'I don't think it's a write-off, but I don't know much about cars.'

He nodded. 'What about the sketch? Let me have a look.'

'I only saw him briefly each time, so I've done my best.'

He sat down next to her. As casually

as her feelings would allow, she turned to him and showed him the drawing.

Stretching his arm across the back of her seat, he took it. He considered the features of the grim, unshaven man. He nodded. 'It looks very good to me. From this picture, he is not someone you'd choose as a friend. Let's deliver this to the main police station and then find somewhere to eat before we leave.'

Anna searched her bag and finally found the battered piece of paper with the policeman's name from the previous day. She gave it to him and he glanced at it.

'Good! They'll deal with us quicker if we've got a name to show them. I forgot to ask the policeman for names this morning.' He stuck the paper in his shirt pocket. He gave her the drawing back and stood up.

He reached for her hand, and she took it. He pulled her gently to her feet. She didn't look in his face, afraid he'd notice the effect he had on her.

They called briefly at the police station. Clearly, it was not a good moment; hardly anyone was available apart from the people in security controls. Showing them the policeman's name, they pointed them in the right direction, but the detective they needed wasn't at his desk either. A colleague eating a sandwich listened to their request for a copy of the report nodded and took Anna's sketch. The man promised to leave the sketch on his colleague's desk with a note. He gave them a copy of the report and noted Isandro's home address and telephone number.

Anna didn't understand very much of the conversation but she trusted Isandro completely. With the report in his hands, they were soon on their way back to his car. They got through the rental company's formalities quickly. Anna signed and they left. It was a relief to get the red tape cleared and out of the way.

'That's enough paperwork for one day. Let's find a shady restaurant. If you sit in the sun, your headache will return.'

*   *   *

They found a friendly restaurant. A colonnade of old trees lined the road and the owner had extended his business onto the pavement outside. The leafy shade helped to provide the right atmosphere for the time of day. Balmy breezes ruffled the checked tablecloths. Anna loved the feeling of being with him, even if only for a brief interlude. There was nothing wrong with liking him or being with him; she just had to be careful that she didn't show him how she felt. Isandro ordered and Anna let him. It was so easy to talk and to be with him. They talked effortlessly about all kind of topics and Anna noticed how well they harmonized. He laughed softly and smiled in all the right places.

'Tell me about yourself.' He bit into a

crunchy piece of buttered soda bread.

'Me? There's nothing special to tell. A very run-of-the-mill existence of growing up, school, university and work.'

'Brothers or sisters?'

'One brother. He's in Australia. Oh, I told you that before, didn't I? I'm fairly sure my parents won't come back until they've seen their first grandchild. Perhaps they'll only come back for my Dad to take early retirement and sell their house — if they stick with their plan to move there.'

'You get on with them?'

She tilted her head to the side. 'Yes. We manage to like each other quite a lot actually.'

'And you'll miss them very much, if they go?'

'It's reassuring to know they're there if something goes wrong in my life but we already live far from one another. That may be why we get on so well. My brother keeps in touch via Skype.'

'Teresa uses Skype too, to keep in touch with my parents. It's amazing, isn't it? When you realize just a century ago it took people months to travel to places like Australia or India, and months for letters to arrive. I haven't used Skype much, but video conferences are run-of-the-mill these days. My parents automatically pass news from Teresa on to me.'

'Do you get on with your parents?'

'Yes, very well.' He leaned back and the chair creaked. He crossed his hand behind his head and looked up into the greenery above them where splotches of sunlight fought their way through the gaps. 'This is the life. No work, good food and good company.'

She skipped the hidden compliment and said, 'Um! Something to remember in winter when the winds freeze my fingers and toes.'

'Winter isn't quite so dramatic hereabouts, but I've often wondered what a snowbound winter is like.'

'Do you've any other brothers or sisters?'

'No, just Teresa and Franco. Teresa is five years older and always bossing me around. Franco's younger. He often found himself in tight spots and needed rescuing before my parents found out what he'd been up to.'

Anna laughed. 'And you were between Teresa, Franco and your parents keeping the peace. Even if Teresa bossed you a lot, you still turned out very well.'

'Did I?' His eyes had a dangerous glint.

Disoriented for a second, she said, 'Yes. I think so, you survived very well.'

He laughed. 'We probably drove my parents mad. Funnily enough, we get on very well nowadays, no matter how much we argued as kids.'

She played with the corner of the serviette. 'Did you always want to be an architect?'

'I didn't know what I wanted to do when school finished. I happened to visit an exhibition by someone called Oscar Niemayer in Paris. Have you ever heard of him?'

'No.'

'He built Brasilia. The exhibition was fascinating. I only went in to look around because it was raining heavily and I happened to be in the vicinity. The photos made me wonder if I would enjoy creating buildings. I never regretted choosing architecture.'

'You seem to like France?'

'I do. I like the French way of life very much, but I love the sun and Spain more.'

Most of the other tables were now empty. The waiter hovered near the doorway waiting for the remaining guests to leave.

Isandro beckoned him and gave him his credit card.

Anna tried to intervene. 'Let me pay! You've helped me so much since yesterday.'

'You've helped me and my family more often. My pleasure!' She gave in as graciously as she could.

14

Once they settled in his car, he drove off and left the busy centre of the town. She enjoyed the feel of the warm wind ruffling her hair.

'Where's your hat?'

'I presume it is still in my car. I had it with me yesterday. It doesn't matter. It wasn't very expensive. I bought it from a kiosk down by the harbour soon after I arrived.'

To her surprise, he stopped on the edge of the town at a small shop and hopped out. He returned with an odd-looking straw hat. It looked drab and dusty and came from some forgotten corner. It now had a questionable shape, but it did its job. Anna felt grateful for the protection it provided, and for his thoughtfulness.

Without a word, he looked sideways at her, bit his lips, spluttered, and burst into laughter. Anna pulled a face and pretended annoyance. He drove on, and Anna decided she felt almost glad she'd had an accident yesterday. Life couldn't be better.

She had nothing to do, so the thoughts whizzed around her mind. She unconsciously started watching the road behind them in the outside mirrors and fidgeting with her bag.

He noticed. 'What's the matter?'

She touched her throat. 'I'm being silly. I'm looking for a strange van.'

He looked across briefly and covered her hands with one of his. He squeezed them. 'Don't worry, Anna. I doubt if he'd be stupid enough to try the same thing twice, especially on a busy road like this one. You're safe with me.' He returned his hand to the steering wheel.

Anna cleared her throat and pretended that his touch hadn't wakened longings.

She leaned back, determined to enjoy the remaining time with him. It went too fast. When he drew up in front of the hotel, she got out reluctantly. Accepting her bag, she looked up into his face and smiled.

'Thanks! Thanks! Thanks! I can't say it often enough. You're my knight in shining armour.'

'I'm not. I'm Isandro Delgado Rodriquez and it's too hot for any kind of armour in Spain.'

She nodded and laughed. 'Well perhaps roasting inside armour isn't very pleasant for a rescuer, but you know what I mean.'

'Hope you have a relaxing shower and a good night's sleep. I'll be in touch.' He considered her for a moment before he leaned forward and put a finger under her chin. Before she'd registered it, he bent and his lips brushed hers. Raising his mouth from hers, he gazed into her eyes before his lips recaptured hers and were more demanding. He tasted wonderful. Anna didn't resist and gave herself willingly to the delight of his kiss. She stared wordlessly, her heart pounding out of control. She longed for him to repeat the experience, but he didn't.

With a voice that betrayed his uncertainty and perhaps his own surprise, he said, 'I hope your boyfriend won't be too upset. Right now, you look like you need a friend to show he cares. I care and I wish all this ugliness hadn't happened.'

His kiss released all kinds of bewildering emotions. She didn't absorb what he said fast enough. He turned away. Smiling weakly, she waited and stood patiently until the engine sprang to life. He looked at her and his dark hair moved in the wind. Anna watched until the jeep reached the street corner and disappeared from her sight.

* * *

She went inside and her hand rose to touch her mouth. Her fingers ran lightly across the surface of her lips. She began to climb the stairs and recalled his words. What had he said about her boyfriend not getting mad? What boyfriend?

★　★　★

She slept securely but still disturbed by the happenings. When she woke, she lay warm and comfortable, and listened. There were the sounds of activity from somewhere below, probably from the kitchen. She also heard the occasional vehicle passing outside, as the village came to life again. She crossed her hands behind her head on the pillow and thought about the situation. His kiss yesterday had complicated the situation for her even more.

Perhaps he wanted to show genuine friendship, but his kiss unleashed more than friendship within her and she wanted more. She didn't intend to pilfer someone else's boyfriend, and she didn't want a clandestine affair either. It was all or nothing for her.

She still had another two weeks of her holiday left. Even when the car-rental people replaced her car, she couldn't imagine driving around the area without feeling nervous anymore. The collision had frightened her. She'd always been careful about picking up hitchhikers, but she'd never honestly reckoned that someone would deliberately try to injure or kill her. As well as grappling with her nerves, she now had to avoid Isandro. She didn't intend to make a fool of herself. She should leave but usually running away never helped anyone. From her point of view, staying wasn't a good alternative either.

★　★　★

Isandro phoned her later that morning and asked her to meet him for a coffee at a small cafe near the harbour.

He was already waiting when she approached. The wind was blustery this morning and it played with the material of her skirt. If he felt disconcerted about his kiss yesterday, it didn't show in his face.

Anna followed his lead, and only a momentary heightened colour showed her nervousness.

'How are you today? Feeling better now you're in familiar surroundings again?'

The waiter came, took their order, and disappeared.

Anna looked out across the masts and rigging of the boats bobbing on the water. 'I didn't think it would bother me, but it does. I'm thinking it would be better for me to leave and not to wait any longer.'

He shifted uneasily and his dark eyes gave nothing away. 'That's understandable, but if you scuttle off, you're letting him win, aren't you? If he scares you off, nothing will suit him better.'

The waiter returned with their coffee.

Anna looked down and stirred the liquid. 'I know, but I won't feel safe exploring on my own anymore. I'm not the type of person who wants to spend time on the beach, each and every day.'

His brows drew together. He looked

very thoughtful. 'Look, give me a day or two to organise something else. I thought you might feel jumpy. I'm going to Barcelona this afternoon. I'll call on an old friend of mine on the way back. He lives off the beaten track. The scenery around his cottage is wild and beautiful. I visit him from time to time. I want you to go home with good memories, not bad ones. His cottage is a great place to relax, and I'm sure Jaime would welcome you. It's what you need to remove any fears before you return home.'

Her head shot up. 'You can't dump me on someone you know out of the blue. Why would he want a visitor, especially a female one? If he's living on his own, why would he enjoy having me around all the time?'

He smiled and Anna found herself smiling back. 'Jaime was my professor. He's not a hermit. He owns a small cottage, here on the coast too, and lives in it in winter. In summer he lives in this little cottage in the mountains.'

'And I expect he simply adores having English visitors thrust on him who can't speak a word of Spanish?'

'I know him quite well. I wouldn't suggest it, unless I thought it would work. He's a widow; his wife died five years ago. They started living in this place up in the hills when he retired. Unfortunately, she died a year later. He kept going because he said they'd planned it together and she would have wanted him to carry on. He speaks excellent English. He worked in Canada for a couple of years.'

He had an answer to everything. 'I still don't feel happy about the idea.'

'Think about it.' He looked at his watch. 'I'll find out how he feels, and we'll talk again tomorrow. The surroundings up there are wild and beautiful. I can imagine you'd enjoy sketching. There's no TV or radio, and cell phones don't work either. You need books or the like to occupy you when daylight fades.'

She was curious. 'What happens if

he's ill or needs help?'

'He has a radio transmitter and says that's all he needs. He goes to Lleida every couple of weeks and has an old jeep that's able to climb straight up the side of a mountain.'

She looked at him sceptically.

He looked at his watch and got up. 'I've got to go. I've got an appointment this afternoon. I'll be in touch.' He looked around for the waiter.

She said, 'Let me pick up the bill, for once. Take care.'

She sat for a while after he left and thought about their conversation. Why did he want to get involved with her problems? She wondered what tomorrow would bring.

* * *

He phoned next day and asked her to come up to the house.

Anna was relieved to find he was alone. She dreaded having Maria around. 'How did your business work out?'

'It was okay. Committees never let you know what they're thinking. At least my design is among the final choices, but it's the most expensive.' Grumpily, he added, 'These days, people consider the costs before they even look at the plans.'

'But you're still in the running; that's a good sign. Clearly, your design impressed them, even if it's more expensive. They would have thrown it out straight away if cost was the only concern.'

He nodded and busied himself making them coffee. Anna stood and watched him. He led the way through the living room and out onto the terrace.

Anna gripped her mug and stared out beyond the balustrade. She took a sip and waited.

He asked, 'And, have you thought about my idea?'

She turned to face him and managed to look unconcerned, even though butterflies were having a rock-and-roll party in her stomach. 'I know that you're being kind, but I don't honestly think it's a good idea to hoist me onto a complete stranger. The notion of somewhere completely different for the last weeks of my holiday is good and tempting but . . .'

'No buts — when I told him about what had happened Jaime said he doesn't want you to leave Spain with bad memories. He remembers very well how friendly and helpful Canadians were. He said he will be glad to welcome you, if you'd like to come. He told me to tell you that his home is very Spartan, but it has a small guest room. As I told you before, the surroundings are delightful. I think it you'd like it and it's just what you need.'

Anna wavered. Her initial nervousness had faded because she felt safe in the familiar surroundings of St. Sabatien. She would get bored if she was confined here for another two weeks. It was also a good idea to put distance between herself and Isandro. Even short meetings with him put her emotions on an all-time high. She wondered why she'd fallen in love with someone she'd only known for a couple of weeks, someone who belonged to another woman.

She decided to follow her instincts. 'Oh, okay; if it makes you happy. And you're absolutely sure your friend won't mind?'

He looked pleased. 'I just told you he'll welcome you with open arms.'

'When can I go, and how do I get there?'

'He told me to bring you anytime I like. The only stipulation is that we stock up with some extra food on the way. An additional mouth to feed would soon demolish his present stores.'

She ran her hands through her hair. 'That goes without saying. Do you have time to take me there?'

'Yes, and I'll pick you up when it's time to leave.'

'Where is this place?'

'It's up where the hills begin to

merge with the mountainous regions, a short distance beyond Lleida. We could stop there to do some shopping in the supermarket.'

She nodded and recalled the journey, the man's attempt to push her off the road, and the ambulance journey to Lleida. 'We pass the place where my car went off the road, don't we? I'd like to take some kind of present for that farmer and his wife, as a small 'thank you' for their help.'

His dark eyes were pools of black velvet. He nodded. 'If you like.'

'What would be suitable?'

He shrugged. 'No idea. Ask your landlady when you warn her you're going away for a couple of days.'

Anna relaxed and decided to enjoy the idea of visiting Isandro's friend.

'When would you like to go?'

'When do you have time to act as my chauffeur?'

'What about tomorrow? You can sort out what you want to take, or leave behind today. As you can imagine, you won't need clothes for festive events. Jaime doesn't have any mod cons like a washing machine, so take note. He takes his stuff down to a laundry in Lleida when he goes shopping. The only alternative is to do things by hand. There's plenty of water because there's a stream behind the house, and Jaime has a small pump so that he doesn't have to fetch it by the bucketfull all the time.'

'It sounds like an adventure.'

'I honestly believe that you'll enjoy it.'

★ ★ ★

When they reached the spot on the road where it had all happened, Anna found that it didn't bother her as much as she had expected.

She pointed to the farmhouse in the distance. 'That's the place. That's where the people live.'

Isandro steered the jeep along the bumpy track to the far-off buildings.

On arrival, they saw the farmer stacking bales of hay in the yard, but he recognized Anna and threw down his fork.

His wife made them stop for coffee and home-made biscuits. Isandro acted as interpreter. They thanked her profusely for her present. She couldn't remember lying on the couch in the small living room or much about any other details. They clearly lived a simple, but satisfying life. They were kind people who hadn't hesitated to help. A short time later, they saw Anna and Isandro off again, waving to them from the yard.

★ ★ ★

The next stop was in a supermarket in Lleida, for groceries. He wandered the shopping aisles alongside her, and told her several times, to stop adding stuff but the trolley soon brimmed over. Anna didn't intend to visit a stranger's home and end up living off his bounty.

She gave Isandro a withering glance and his protests lessened. With her boxes of groceries and a box of Spanish red wine stacked in the back of the jeep, they drove on.

* * *

The road climbed gradually through austere scenery. Boulders, large and small, and interspersing sparse vegetation spread across the landscape. Eventually Isandro veered off the road. The mountains in the distance reached up to a cloudless sky. He drove across the rough ground along a barely conspicuous track. It rounded the foot of a mountain and reared off to the left. The landscape began to look less hostile, although Anna still couldn't see any kind of habitation. Isandro's jeep sent the frightened sheep scattering in all directions whenever they drew closer. Anna bounced in her seat on their way downhill towards a small wooded territory. She guessed there must be a river, or some kind of water supply close by, otherwise it wouldn't look so green. The surrounding scenery looked awe inspiring and majestic. She already itched to get her impressions down on paper.

15

She looked closely at the small solid building as they approached. The windows were small, the roof overhung the white stone walls, and the blue door was wide open. When the jeep halted, Isandro leapt down and called, 'Jaime!' They waited but no one appeared. Isandro started to show her around. A slanted extension to the cottage contained a supply of wood, and a smaller room turned out to be the toilet. Anna wrinkled her nose but smiled.

They walked around the side of the house and Anna heard a stream bubbling. She saw a small plot of cleared ground containing tubs of vegetables. There were tomatoes, paprika, beans clambering upwards on supportive sticks, eggplants, zucchini, spring onions and fresh bunches of lettuce in a small cold-frame. Anna looked on with interest and commented, 'He doesn't need to buy any vegetables. It looks like he's self-supporting.'

Isandro nodded. 'He grows all these vegetables because he has plenty of water from the stream. He buys what he can't grow himself. I think potatoes are no-go items, and things like carrots and onions. Don't ask me why, I don't know. I presume the ground is wrong for root vegetables. I'm sure Jaime will explain if you're interested.'

They found a weatherworn bench bordering the garden and sat down.

The sound of goats and sheep in the far distance was all they heard for a while, and then some heavy steps from around the other side of the house interrupted the peaceful atmosphere. A brown shaggy dog of indeterminate age preceded its owner and he eyed them carefully. He decided they presented no danger to his master.

Jamie had a thin face and bushy grey eyebrows. He was slightly bent and his eyes were set closely together and dark in colour. His mouth widened into a smile as he spotted the two of them.

He walked unhurriedly towards them and Isandro stood up. The older man embraced Isandro and slapped him on the back. They exchanged greetings in Spanish and then the man turned to Anna.

'So! This is Anna. Hello Anna! I'm looking forward to your company for a while.' He spoke excellent English and she could still hear a slight Canadian twang. His hair was thin on top but he still had astonishingly good white teeth.

'Anna, this is my friend Jaime.'

'Thank you for having me. I hope I won't get in your way. We've just been admiring your garden.'

Jaime glanced briefly in the direction of the vegetables. 'I like having fresh food. It keeps me occupied, and it tastes much better than the shop stuff.'

Anna bent down to fondle the dog's ears. He had placid brown eyes. The dog decided to like this new visitor; she had a soft voice.

Isandro told him, 'Your front door is open.'

'Isandro my friend, have you seen anyone else near here? Anyway, I've nothing worth pinching. Strangers hardly ever come this far without a good reason. Local shepherds call sometimes for a cup of coffee if they're in the area, but visitors are rare. Talking of coffee, let's have some!' He asked him, 'Are you staying the night?'

'If you can squeeze me in.'

The knowledge that Isandro intended to stay for a while pleased her. Among other reasons, it gave her more time to get used to her host before Isandro left her to return home. Anna wondered if Maria was angry that Isandro had gone to so much trouble to make her remaining holiday an agreeable time. Probably.

'You'll have to manage with the living-room couch. It should just about be long enough for you.'

'I'll manage. We've brought half the

shop with us. Anna insisted. We've also bought a couple of boxes of wine and some fresh chicken and steaks.'

Jaime smiled at Anna. 'A woman after my own heart. I've smoked meat and plenty of tinned meat too, but fresh meat is a luxury for me most of the time. It's something I really appreciate.'

He led the way. Inside the rooms were tiny and Isandro filled more than his share of the available space. The small cottage contained a kitchen-cum-living-room and two bedrooms leading off the main room. Jaime opened the door of one and said with a flourish,

'Your domain for the length of your stay.'

'Thank you. It looks lovely.' She noticed the blob of colour on the windowsill and said, 'How thoughtful — some flowers.'

'My wife always said flowers welcome guests. She was right. Out here the choice is modest, but wild flowers have a special charm.'

'They're lovely. All our so-called

cultivated flowers come from their wild forms. Nothing could be nicer and more fitting in this room. I hope I haven't put you to any trouble?'

His eyes twinkled. 'No, not at all. Everything is very Spartan as you see, but if you need anything and think I can help, just ask.'

Anna nodded. She stood her suitcase at the foot of the narrow bed with its white linen sheets and pillowcases. 'I'll unpack later. Can I help you with the coffee?'

Jaime's face melted into a buttery smile and shook his head. Anna sensed that she'd like this man.

Jaime made them coffee, and afterwards Isandro said he'd take her to his favourite spot. She loved being alone with him, although she knew it was a form of self-punishment; he belonged to someone else. She followed him across the stream, through the bordering wood and out the other side across some open countryside.

Anna found that the landscape had a sort of haunting bleakness, but with Isandro at her side, it didn't bother her much. Peace and quiet reigned all around them. Far in the distance, and up above them, grey clouds covered the mountain peaks.

Isandro looked cheerful. As they walked, Anna thought about how strong-minded he was, and that he was also intelligent, capable, and kinder than he wanted anyone to suspect.

She followed him up an incline via a barely noticeable footpath. After a couple of minutes, he branched off towards a ledge of rock. It overlooked the surrounding countryside and gave them a spectacular view. Spots of dark birds circled in the sky far above them. He flopped down and she joined him. He gestured at the view.

'Quite something, don't you agree?'

She nodded.

He bent one leg, encircled his arms

around it, and looked across at her. 'Have you decided about going to Australia?'

She shook her head. She hadn't thought about Australia for days. She suddenly reflected that it could provide her with a way out. If she went, it might help her to forget him faster. On the other side of the world there would be no temptation to find out what he was doing, or even to see him again. 'Not yet.' She pushed her hair out of her face. 'I can't leave my job without giving notice, even if I wanted to. They like people to leave at the end of the school year unless there is an urgent reason.'

He plucked a stem of grass and chewed on it absent-mindedly. 'Are your parents definitely staying in Australia?'

She shrugged. 'They haven't said so yet. I'm not going to worry about something that may never happen.' She breathed deeply. The smell of sun and grass drifted around them and filled her lungs with fragrant fresh air.

'You already said you didn't see why

you should give up your life here, just to start from scratch all over again there. Be honest and don't compromise to suit other people, even your own parents. Life is too short for compromises.'

'Are you always so honest about everything, private and professional?'

'I try to be honest with myself, and with others. That doesn't always make me popular, but I'm not interested in being popular. It is easier to live with than half-truths, and far less demanding. If you spend your life compromising, you just waste your time. You don't really want to go to Australia, do you? You've no guarantee that your life will be any better if you go. Why go?'

'Yes, I know what you mean. It's just the idea of the rest of the family being so far away. I have friends, but a family is something different; it's always a rock in a storm.' She changed the direction of the conversation. 'This is a wonderful spot to do some drawing.'

'I thought you might like it.' He gazed into her face and Anna swallowed a lump in her throat.

'Did you always want to be a teacher?'

'No, at one time I dreamed of becoming a book illustrator — of children's books.'

'And you didn't follow your dream?'

Anna had almost forgotten her dream. She shook her head. 'The competition is savage. There are few books to illustrate, and hundreds of illustrators. In the end I opted for a steady income. It wasn't the wrong decision because I like children and I like teaching.'

'But that's not exactly the same as achieving your dream.'

She laughed softly. 'We can't all achieve our dreams. I like my job and I still enjoy excursions into the world of art. I visit museums, and go to as many exhibitions as I can.' She tilted her head. 'Perhaps I should have sent publishers some examples of my work.'

He got to his feet and held out his hand. 'You still can! You draw well, and you know all about children. I imagine that's a perfect combination to produce book illustrations. Look! The sun is going down; Jaime will wonder where we are. Are you ready?'

'Of course!' She took his hand and black eyes met grey ones as he pulled her gently to her feet. She desperately needed more of him than his hand but she let go because he must never know how much. He went ahead down the narrow pathway and she busied herself with her own thoughts.

* * *

By the time they reached the cottage and helped Jaime prepare the evening meal, the sun had almost disappeared. The three of them shared a simple but delicious meal and then sat outside under the overhang roof, sharing a bottle of wine. The moon broke out from behind the clouds and some insects were buzzing around. They irritated, but didn't sting, so Anna tried to ignore them. Listening to the two men, it was clear that they liked each other. Jaime also knew all about Isandro's family, because he asked after Teresa, Franco and their parents.

As the nearby trees darkened into solid black silhouettes, Anna looked up at countless bright stars in the sky. She remarked, 'The skies are fantastic but it is cooler here than it is down at the coast.'

Isandro asked, 'Are you cold? Want to borrow my sweater? I can leave it here.'

'No, I'm fine. I brought one of my own. I just mean the temperatures are different.'

Jaime leaned back against the rough white stonework. 'Umm! You're right. It is cooler here because we're closer to the mountains. During the day, it's very pleasant, but it cools down at night. Some days I light a fire to take the edge off the chill. When autumn arrives, it's too cold. The shepherds take their flocks down to lower levels and I go back to my house on the coast. I can't leave anything here that absorbs moisture. I pack some things, like the mattresses, into air-tight bags, and take loads of other vulnerable items with me.'

'It explains why you have piles of wood in the outhouse.'

He laughed. 'Yes, for cooler temperatures. I gather it when out walking. Sometimes a tree has fallen over because of age or illness; sometimes branches are blown off in stormy weather. They provide me with fire-wood.'

'Who owns the land?'

'The regional authorities. I own this little piece. I bought it from a shepherd. His family lived here for generations, but none of his children wanted to carry on, so eventually he moved to town. Someone told me he owned this place and was willing to sell it.' His eyes twinkled brightly in the dark. 'There are strict building regulations hereabouts.

You can't erect a new building. You can't alter the outward appearance of the ones already in place either. They're trying to keep the environment unchanged. Anyway, not many people want to settle anywhere without modern-day facilities, so I don't think there's any danger of weekend tourists running riot, or people wanting holiday homes out here. My wife and I saw this place years and years ago when we were hiking. We never forgot it. It was run-down in appearance even in those days. By the time I traced its owner the roof was almost non-existent. My wife and I spent an enjoyable summer putting in back into a habitable condition. Someone helped professionally with the roof, and digging a pit for the toilet, but apart from that we sorted it out on our own.'

'I bet that it wasn't as easy as it sounds. It is very isolated, isn't it? What if you need a special screw or you need sandpaper? It's half a day's journey to Lleida, there and back.'

He laughed and absent-mindedly stroked the head of his dog. 'Exactly! So you learn to improvise and do things like straightening nails or making replacements to save unnecessary trips.'

Anna sighed and said, 'This is a place for being, not doing. It's perfect.' Anna thought about Jaime. He lived alone, an austere and Spartan life, but he was one of the most contented, uncomplicated people she'd ever met.

They sat staring into the darkness and chatting until the cool air drove them indoors. Sometimes Isandro and Jaime talked about people, places and topics she knew nothing about, but Anna didn't mind. She enjoyed the atmosphere and she already liked Jaime. She loved Isandro.

* * *

Anna woke to the sound of someone moving around outside. Sunlight poured into the small bedroom and it warmed her face and skin. She hadn't slept so

212

well for days. The change of surround-ings and the mountain air already had a beneficial effect. She knelt to look out of the tiny window set into the thick walls. Jaime was outside, the dog lying nearby. He was busy in his vegetable garden. Jaime must get up with the dawn. She struggled to open the window and the fresh air rushed in. Jaime looked up and smiled. She waved.

Anna discovered later that Jaime was orderly. Nothing had forced him to act in that way; he just believed everyone ought to have some kind of structure in their daily efforts. He and his wife had decided together to split their lives between the small house on the coast and this place in the summer. They'd done so to be close to nature and to come to terms with their own short-comings.

Jumping out of bed, she washed quickly using the old-fashioned jug and washbasin on the small commode. Dressed in jeans and a short-sleeved

T-shirt, she opened the door carefully. Isandro lay untidily on the long leather couch. She tiptoed and stopped briefly to consider his face. She noted the shadow of a beard, and long dark eyelashes brushing the top of his thin cheeks. If she bent down, she could have easily kissed him. She didn't, but butterflies flapped around in her stomach as she stared at him.

She went towards the door, careful not to make a sound. The well-oiled door opened into the freshness of the morning. After a few seconds of admiring the outlook, she walked around the side and into the vegetable garden. Jaime was nowhere in sight, but she heard his voice. Following it, she found him talking to a handful of chickens in a pen.

'Morning Jaime! I didn't see those yesterday.'

'They were probably already inside when you arrived. They get up with the first streak of dawn, and settle down long before daylight fades away. They have their own position on the perches and if they don't claim theirs early enough, one of the others will pinch it, and they get very het up about that. The latecomers have to make do with the end spot. Their concern is an inborn instinct. The one on the end will be first to go if a predator gets in during the night.'

Anna laughed. 'A kind of perch pecking-order! Isandro is still asleep. Can I help you?'

'You are not here to work. You can help with the evening meal if you like, but otherwise your time is your own. Isandro said you like sketching?'

'Um! I studied art, but I decided I didn't have enough talent to make a living from it. Then I trained to be a teacher. I'm still fiercely enthusiastic about art, although I love teaching. I don't have much time to indulge in painting or sketching anymore, but I at least try to keep my hand in when I'm on holiday.'

'Perhaps the scenery here will inspire

you. Have you been to any of the famous Spanish art museums? We've some real gems.'

'Yes, I know. I intended to take a trip to Barcelona to see the Joan Miro gallery but time has almost run out. It will have to wait until next time.'

'The Picasso museum is worth a visit too and there's another good museum of contemporary art in Barcelona. You'll see them next time round, I hope. I've just been persuading these ladies to let me have a couple of extra eggs for our breakfast this morning.'

Anna viewed the well-fed group and their proud cockerel eying them from a distance. 'And they agreed to your request without a fight?'

Jaime opened his hands and displayed three big brown eggs. He winked. 'I'll be back to pinch the rest when they're out busy scratching for worms. They run free during the day, and so far I've never lost one.' He looked at his watch. 'Let's tip Isandro out of bed. We'll never have breakfast if we show him mercy for too long. He tucked his arm through hers and they went back to the house.

★ ★ ★

Isandro stood in the doorway, stretching. He wore some old jeans and a washed-out T-shirt.

Anna wondered if he'd borrowed something from Jaime, but he looked too well-muscled and powerful to fit into Jaime's clothes.

Anna had never been more conscious of his tall, athletic physique but she managed a casual, 'Morning!'

His eyes twinkled. 'Morning! It looks like I'm last up. I hope it is still morning. Where have you been?'

'Pinching chickens' eggs.'

'How reprehensible. Still, one of Jaime's fresh eggs to start the day is a good idea. I'll just pay a visit to the house around the corner and have a wash.' He disappeared inside, and reappeared almost immediately with a towel. Anna had rarely seen him so relaxed and her love blossomed stronger than ever.

★ ★ ★

Breakfast was enjoyable. They ate outdoors on a rough plank table and backless benches. They had smoked bacon, fried eggs, tomatoes, and strong coffee that left a slightly bitter taste on the tongue. Jaime also presented them with some delicious goat's cheese that was creamy and sharp. He explained local shepherds always brought him some when they called.

They took their time finishing the meal. Anna didn't want it to end.

Isandro looked at his watch eventually and admitted that he ought to leave. 'Unfortunately, they are insisting on slight adjustments to my design by tomorrow morning. As long as the basic design remains, I'll play along, but I won't make any radical changes to alter the overall appearance. I'll see how they react!' He reflected, 'Perhaps it'd be a good idea for me to go straight to Barcelona. How can I contact you, Jaime?'

Anna reflected that Maria waited in Barcelona.

Jaime went indoors and came back with a piece of paper. 'That's the telephone number and name of the chap I contact in Lleida. If I need to phone you or you want to tell me something, you just get in touch with him.'

Isandro stuffed the paper into his jeans' pocket. 'I'll get my bits and pieces.' It took just minutes until he returned. Anna noticed he still had a shadow of a beard, so he intended to postpone a shave until sometime later.

She and Jaime walked with him to where he'd parked his jeep.

She looked up at him, the sun at his back, casting shadows on his face. 'Drive carefully.' She didn't know what else to say.

'I will. I think you'll enjoy your stay with this old rascal.'

'Hey, watch your tongue! If I'd realized that you'd turn out so shameless and impertinent, I wouldn't have given you such good marks at university.'

Isandro laughed and kept his eyes on Anna. 'Enjoy yourself. If you want to leave earlier, Jaime can phone his friend and I'll come and get you. If not I'll definitely come back to fetch you in time.'

She nodded with a knot in her throat. She didn't know what else to say so she just stood and waited for him to start the engine. It sprang to life, cutting the silence and sending some birds into a flurry. He drove off, still waving a hand above his head. Anna remained cemented to the spot until she could see and hear the jeep no longer.

★　★　★

Jaime turned away and went back to the table. He began to stack the breakfast dishes. He wondered if he imagined things when he looked at Anna still standing there and looking into the distance.

16

Accustomed to constant sounds and people everywhere, Anna needed a little time to adjust to the isolation and silence. She'd never stayed in such an uninhabited place before. At first, she stuck close to the house. Jaime noticed her reaction, but didn't comment. She sketched close to the cottage. Gradually she began to enjoy the tranquillity of the place. Jaime took her on walks and she climbed the nearby slopes with him. The impressive scenery and the invigorating air were perfect for making her forget the van and its driver.

He insisted that she didn't do any of his daily chores, although they prepared the evening meal together. She made a cake one day when he translated the ingredients from an old cookery book. The speed that it disappeared implied that it turned out very well.

Scenes of one of her favourite spots, the vegetable garden, soon filled several pages in her sketch book. A natural spring surfaced somewhere on the edge of the wood. It became a brook and that gurgled and bubbled its way along the edge of the vegetable patch to disappear beneath a gathering of boulders further along the way. Its water was transparent and ice-cold. The further she wandered from the house, the more brittle the surrounding sparse vegetation and grass seemed. The lack of water made nature's job difficult.

* * *

Anna decided the place was remote but interesting and fascinating. It gave her an insight into how simple life could be. The scenery soon began to stimulate her fantasy. Anna began to understand why Jaime and his wife had chosen this spot to spend the evening of their lives. On reflection, she was sad that they'd only shared their mutual dream for such a short time. Anna told him so one evening when the oil lamps were glowing softly and the wind outside fretted the shutters.

He looked without seeing and shrugged. 'I didn't believe I could ever stay married to the same woman all my life before I met Julia. I'm grateful for every single second we had together. I wish she were here. Not a day passes without me thinking about her a hundred times. Sometimes I still talk to her out loud.'

'Did you know instantly she was the one?'

'You mean love at first sight?' He paused. 'No. Sometimes people walk into your life and they're there, and you don't see them, until one day, everything falls into place and suddenly you feel breathless every time you look at them. Julia taught in a junior school, like you. We met at various get-togethers frequently because one of her brothers worked as an assistant at the university.' He took a sip of wine. 'I'd had several affairs long before I met her but nothing that ever lasted beyond physical euphoria. Gradually I admitted I needed something more permanent, something I hadn't found in any woman till then. I suddenly realized Julia possessed what I yearned for. My previous girlfriends were always extravagant and outrageous and she was different. She possessed plenty of self-confidence but also had an aura of understanding and gentleness about her that defies description. I found part of myself when I found her. She nullified my restlessness and brought me peace. I think she dodged me for a long time, because she'd heard all the gossip about the young, amorous professor.' He shrugged. 'Understandable. Her brothers complicated things too because they didn't trust me and guarded her like the Crown Jewels.'

'And then?'

'Then something fell into place and we began to talk a lot. The attraction grew every time we met. I never talked as much to a woman before, or since.

When I made up my mind she was the one for me, I had trouble persuading her family I was serious. Only Julia's determination, once she'd made up her mind, finally got us to the altar and kept us in touch with her family.'

'Isandro told me she died soon after you began to divide your lives between here and the coast.'

He shifted uneasily. 'Yes, that was a damnable stroke of fate. I only thank God that she didn't suffer very long. She would have hated to end up an invalid or a burden to anyone. I only wish I could have gone with her, but I have to wait my time. I'm sure her spirit is still with me, every single day.'

Anna had a lump in her throat as she considered Jaime. 'Any children?'

He cleared his throat a little. 'Yes, a daughter. She's married and living in Madrid. Her husband is a dentist. I like him. Elena is like Julia, not in looks, but she has many of Julia's habits and gestures. They want me to move to Madrid and I probably will one day, when I notice that I'm no longer able to cope on my own. When the time comes, I'll miss this place like hell. Staying in the house on the coast isn't problematic. There are plenty of people around all the time. That would be possible even in old age. In contrast, I'm isolated here. A big city does have compensations and sometimes I miss the theatre, concerts, and exhibitions. If I move to a city, that would be the main compensation for giving up something as perfect as this cottage in the wilderness. Perhaps I'll die first; that would be fine with me. Whatever God decides.'

★ ★ ★

After a couple of days, Anna grew more adventurous and went further afield. Jaime took her to spots where there were wonderful views of the surrounding countryside. Sometimes he stayed for a while watching her sketch and giving her encouragement. Sometimes he left her and went off looking for one of the shepherds he knew was in the vicinity. He usually came back with some crumbly, creamy cheese.

One evening they were both sitting in the much-used and extremely comfortable armchairs. Anna had a book in her hand, and Jaime was listening to some classical music playing in the background. The portable hi-fi ran on batteries and it was one of Jaime's few luxuries. He didn't listen regularly, but when he did, Anna had the feeling it meant a great deal to him.

Jaime's voice floated above a Beethoven's symphony. 'When did you meet Isandro?'

Anna put down her book and told him.

Jaime chuckled. 'Trust Isandro. However, that house is really something, isn't it? When he told me he'd bought the plot of land, I wondered what he'd make out of it, but it's close to perfection. The building hasn't made any difference to the environment. You can hardly see it from the road or from the sides either. Despite its ultra-modern design, it doesn't stick out like a sore thumb. It's almost part of the natural rock. You'd need to come very close to pick out the details from the water side. He hasn't taxed nature's patience too much. The whole concept is very clever.'

'Yes. It's lovely. I like the way all the rooms have windows looking out over the water. The furnishings are all minimal and blend with each other and their surroundings beautifully. It's very impressive. I don't know enough about architecture to understand the difficulties, but I'm sure they were boundless.' She paused. 'Was Isandro a good student?'

Jaime nodded. 'I'd never tell him so to his face, but he was the best of his year. He never compromised, even as a student. He spent more time arguing with his teachers about some radical idea, or what was right or wrong, than he did producing designs.

Most students tend to give in when their professors tell them what to do, and how to do it. They end up as average architects. They produce good work, but don't have the fire in their belly to produce something outstanding.'

'So you think he'll go to the top?'

He nodded. 'With luck and some encouragement. Even if someone produces out-of-the-ordinary designs, he still needs a special kind of character to push his conception through to the very end. Any new design is essentially a risk. No one can really imagine what a building will be like until it stands. Drawings, pictures, computer animations are good, but the feeling a building conveys is only evident when it's finally up and in position. To get attention-grabbing commissions, you eventually need a name — a world-renowned name. That, and a good reputation, is hard to make these days. A lot of talented architects end up working for other famous architects because that's the only way they can satisfy their own aspirations.'

'Isandro appears happy with what he's doing. I know that he's working on several projects at present. Teresa told me recently that someone wants him to build something out in the wilderness and he's entered a design for a new museum annex.'

'Yes, I know about that. He's busy these days. I wish him luck. His success is growing and his name will spread eventually. If he sticks to his principles, sooner or later things will take off of their own accord.'

'And you chose to live in a very simple cottage out in the wilderness? If you spent your life with constructions and special architectural designs, isn't life here an extreme contrast?'

He laughed. 'Perhaps, but a cottage like this one is the simplest form of a dwelling place. It has a simple construction and it fills fundamental needs. It shelters and provides security. Anyone can own something bigger and full of luxury, but it's a challenge to accept the minimum that life offers, and still be contented with your lot. Do you like Isandro?'

The question was unexpected and disconcerted her for a moment. Anna coloured. 'Yes of course. He's been a good friend, especially since the episode with that van.'

'He told me about that. That was a nasty business. He said he felt responsible because the trouble started with the break-in at his house.'

'I keep telling him he's not responsible. It was just bad luck.'

'It isn't easy to persuade him to change his beliefs. In one way, I'm almost glad. If it hadn't happened, we wouldn't have met.'

★　★　★

Next day Anna disappeared to sketch from a favourite spot. Jaime sat outside on the bench and suddenly noticed there was a vehicle coming round the edge of the hill. He watched it with interest and soon recognised Isandro's jeep. Isandro visited him from time to time but now he wondered if Anna was the main attraction. His mouth curved into a smile. A few minutes later, the jeep stopped in a cloud of dust and Isandro jumped out.

Without his usual greeting, he looked around and said urgently, 'Where's Anna?'

'She's out sketching. I think she went to that outcrop of rock on the far side of the steep slope on *Roca Gris*. Do you know where I mean? What's the matter? You look worried.'

Isandro ran a hand down his face. 'I've a feeling that someone has been watching me, and has been for a day or so. This morning I decided to visit you two. On the far side of Lleida, I noticed a car was following me.'

'A car? Not a van?' 'No, a car, a blue Ford. I kept it in sight and deliberately pulled into that petrol station just before one gets to Lleida. The Ford drove on. I managed a brief look at the driver, and he looked like Anna's sketch. He must have turned off down a sidetrack and waited. When I resumed the journey a short time later, he was suddenly behind me again. He kept a distance between us, but I'm certain he was following.'

'And? What did you do?'

'I pulled into the side and phoned the police before my phone lost contact with the net. Luckily, I had the number of the detective in Lleida in my wallet. When I explained he ran the car number through the computer. It must have matched something because he said he'd come here to make sure Anna was safe. Apparently, the police did circulate Anna's sketch around the petrol stations, banks. A couple of people reported that they'd seen him recently. I warned the detective a normal car won't cope with the terrain and he needed a 4WD. He said he needed special permission to use one of their off-road vehicles, but promised to meet me here as soon as he could.'

'Why would anyone strange want to follow you?'

'I presume that he wants to find Anna. She's the only person who can identify him with certainty, if they ever catch him and his colleague. Most likely, he wants to frighten her into not giving evidence against him. There's no official road down here, just a barely visible track leading off the highway. I made sure the Ford wasn't in sight, and then piled a heap of stones, before I left the road at the turn-off. I told the detective I would mark it that way. Luckily he's a local man and knows the area well, so he'll probably spot a pile of stones sooner than a stranger would.'

'And he thinks it's worth the trip out here? That doesn't sound very reassuring.' Jaime looked in the direction of the main road.

They decided not to upset Anna.

'Let's wait and see what happens first. Perhaps you are worrying for no reason.'

Isandro still concentrated on carefully inspecting the track and the surrounding countryside. 'Perhaps, but that Ford was following me, and the man looked like Anna's picture. I'm sure of that. I don't like it one little bit.'

'When did you lose sight of it?'

'Soon after I left Lleida. There's never much traffic on the road after Lleida. He would be clever enough to keep back and not to get too close. There are quite a few curves so I presume he caught up every time he thought I'd rounded one of them.'

'He doesn't actually know if Anna can give a recognizable description of him, or not, does he?'

Isandro shrugged. 'I assume he's just not taking any chances.'

Jaime's eyes travelled the familiar terrain. 'Well, I can't see anything unusual at the moment. I'll make us some coffee.'

Isandro glanced back in the direction of the highway and then followed him into the house with his holdall.

***

In the distance, just around the bend and out of sight, a blue car threw up a cloud of dust as it left the highway and began its downward decent.

***

Isandro dropped his holdall on the couch, and Jaime made some coffee. The two men went outside again with their mugs.

'I've brought fresh groceries with me.'

'Jaime nodded and took a sip of coffee.

Isandro asked, 'How are you and Anna getting on?'

'We like each other. She's natural, sympathetic, helpful and undemanding, a thoroughly nice young woman. I think the isolation bothered her at first but she goes off on her own for hours at a time now.'

'That's what I hoped she'd do. This business has damaged her self-confidence a bit. It wouldn't have happened if she hadn't been in my house on the night of the burglary.'

'If, if . . . the world is full of ifs. Don't waste time thinking about it. It's fate, or chance, or whatever you decide to call it. If it hadn't happened, you probably wouldn't know her as well as you do. That would be a pity, wouldn't it?'

Isandro looked into the distance. 'Yes, that's very true.'

'What about your museum complex? Have they decided yet?'

Isandro shook his head. 'No, but they're in the final stages of deciding.'

'I had a letter from Juan Cortez. He's working for an office in Marseille.'

Isandro took a sip of coffee. 'Really? He had some good ideas. I hope his bosses don't smother his creativity.'

They continued to talk about mutual acquaintances and kept their eyes on the surroundings.

'What time does Anna usually come back?'

'It varies, according to how much she

sketches. She's not an outstanding talent, but she captures things very well. Her sketches are very interesting. She says herself that she could never make her living from art and she has never considered doing so. She enjoys what she does, and perhaps that gives her more satisfaction in the long run.'

'She likes teaching, so art isn't so important anymore. I saw how she handled Teresa's two kids. Ina and Eduardo liked her straight away. She likes her job and it shows. I like her attitude too.'

'Yes, I agree. What about your television presenter? Elena or was it Maria? I thought you'd bring her here one day.'

He gave a derisive laugh. 'If Maria can't have a shower twice a day, go out somewhere for her meals every night, spend a fortune on cosmetics and clothes, life would have no meaning. I've finally woke up and realized we don't have the same aims or ideals. Life isn't just about achieving fame, is it? It's about who you are and what is good for you.'

'Oh ho! That's a change of thinking. I can remember how you revelled in having the attention of every female student on the campus. Your long-term aims were riches and fame, as I remember.'

'Other times, other places! Experience makes fools and monarchs of us all.'

'And what are you now, a fool or a monarch?'

'I'm not sure myself.' Isandro threw the last dregs of coffee in an arc onto the ground in front of the cottage. He looked at his watch. 'I think I'll go to meet Anna. It's a good idea for her to have company until we know there's no danger.'

'You'll surprise her, but I think it'll be a pleasant surprise. I'll be here if the police turn up, or to greet any other unwelcome visitors.'

'I'll change my shoes first.'

Jaime picked up the mugs and went

to wash them in the stream. He met Isandro on his return.

Isandro crossed the stream and headed through the wood.

Jaime sat on the bench; Pedro, his dog, settled down for a siesta next to him.

★ ★ ★

The light showed greenish under the trees and golden sunshine fought its way between the leaves. The sun landed in speckled patches on the ground beneath. Somewhere behind him, he heard the chickens bickering and the sound echoed through the wood. His mind still circled around the Ford car and he hoped it would be an unnecessary trip for the detective. A layer of dried leaves dampened his footsteps and he soon reached the outer edge. Once there, he set out across open country and then undertook a gradual upward climb. The hill grew steeper and he detoured to the side and found

Anna. She sat on an outcrop and staring out across the landscape. Her sketchpad lay on her lap and she looked lost in thought. For a few seconds he stopped and watched her. He coughed and broke the spell.

Anna jumped and looked up. Seeing him so unexpectedly confused her. Her colour heightened but she automatically smiled with pleasure. 'Isandro! What a nice surprise. I didn't expect to see you. In fact, I didn't expect anyone. When did you arrive?'

He looked relaxed. The wind had messed his hair. He looked young although his expression was not wholly untroubled.

'Not long ago. I had a cup of coffee with Jaime and then came to collect you.' He lowered himself and made himself comfortable next to her.

His nearness made her nervous. She tried to hide it. Anna put her sketchpad aside and wrapped her arms around her knees. Looking at the scenery, she said, 'I love this place. The peace and the intactness of nature are perfect.'

'I agree wholeheartedly. That's why I like coming here too.' He bent one knee, rested his hand on it, and stuck the other out in a straight line. He looked at her sketchbook. 'You've been busy?'

She laughed softly. 'Yes. I've been trying to capture the atmosphere and the scenery. I'm not sure if I succeeded but I'll find that out in the middle of winter when I start to fill in the pages.'

He reached forward. 'May I?'

She snatched the pad and clasped it tightly to her chest. 'It's for my eyes only. You're too critical.'

'I won't criticize, promise. I've seen your drawings before. You're good.'

She shook her head determinedly. Anna didn't want him to see one page in particular. She'd tried to draw him from memory and she didn't want him to see it, or to have to explain why he was among all the others in there. 'Perhaps, one day before I leave.' She put it away, and leaned back, using her arms as a support. She looked across the windswept land. 'You'd be stupid not to see this and realize how superfluous human beings are. The human race could die out tomorrow but nature would carry on.'

'Yes. Makes you think, doesn't it?'

They sat there for a time in companionable silence until Anna said, 'It's a lonely life for Jaime in his cottage, but he doesn't seem to mind.'

He considered her for a moment and then shrugged. 'He's not lonely. He's content with his lot and with nature. I'm sure he'll stay here as long as he can manage. Do you want to go on drawing?'

'No, we may as well go back. I expect Jaime is already planning our meal, and I like to help.' She stuffed her pad into the satchel. 'It's the only thing he lets me do.'

★   ★   ★

Isandro pushed himself to a standing position and reached out for her hand.

Unable to avoid it, she placed her hand in his and he pulled her up. Just his touch sent her emotions haywire. She bent down to pick up the canvas bag and he set off round the curve of the slope. Anna followed. Going downhill, the grass was dry and smooth. She was more careful, she'd slipped a couple of times.

Once they were on flatter ground, Isandro carried on with long, purposeful strides. Anna didn't try to catch up. He was busy with his own thoughts and didn't notice how the distance between them lengthened. When they reached the edge of the wood, he did look around and he noticed he'd left her behind. He smiled and waited. Anna's pulse galloped out of control.

Slightly out of breath, Anna called to him. 'Carry on! I think I know the way almost better than you do by now.'

He grinned and shrugged before he disappeared between gnarled trunks of the trees.

17

Walking slowly through the wood, the only sounds Anna heard were her own feet crunching on dried leaves and, even though she couldn't see him, the almost faint sound of Isandro walking ahead. When a figure popped out from behind a tree to block her path, the shock almost rocked her physically. Her pulse zoomed to dizzy heights when she recognized it was the burglar. Her hand flew to her throat.

He noticed her reaction and a leering grin spread across his face as he recognized her mounting panic. He ranted at her in rapid Spanish. She stared at him, feeling paralyzed. He was loud, aggressive and his facial expression was threatening. He thought she was Spanish. He waited for her to answer. She felt numb with shock but forced herself to think of how to escape.

Isandro's footsteps had faded away. He must be on the other side of the wood by now. He would cross the stream and reach the cottage believing she was following right behind him. She buried her fears and tried to look as if she understood him. Frantically, she figured out there was enough room between the two of them for her to make a dash for it. If she could avoid him, she'd run like billy-o. If he caught her, she'd scream as loudly as possible and hope that Isandro would hear.

Anna waited, watching the man's angry gestures and listening to a hostile torrent of words. Distracted for a moment by the sound of some birds flapping in nearby trees, he looked up and she decided it was now or never. Throwing her satchel aside, she veered to the side and ran. He tried to grab her, but she dodged out of reach. Anna sprinted, avoiding trees, charging through the undergrowth, and breathing short gasps of air as she kept going. She had one decided advantage over him. She knew the wood well, and which direction to take. Somehow, she kept ahead of him even though he was bigger and stronger. He stumbled and lurched through the unfamiliar terrain as he tried to close the gap. He swore at her but Anna saw she was nearing the edge of the wood and the light between the trees grew stronger. When she broke into the clearing, she almost ran straight into Isandro.

★   ★   ★

'What the . . . ' He got no further because the man crashed through the shrubs behind her. He recognised him from Anna's sketch and he shoved Anna behind him.

The man halted and panted. He considered the two of them and threw a barrage of Spanish at Isandro. Isandro's reply sounded even more aggressive.

Still trying to get her breath, Anna felt safe just to be with him again.

Isandro muttered, 'Anna, go to

Jaime! I'll deal with this.'

Reluctantly, she knew if he had to protect her, and deal with the burglar at the same time, it lessened his chances. 'I'll fetch Jaime. Two are better than one. Don't let him hurt you.' She backed away and fled across the clearing. Jumping the stream, she looked back and saw the man still facing Isandro and coming towards him.

★   ★   ★

She raced through the vegetable patch and round the corner of the house. Jaime was sat on the bench. Breathless, she explained and pointed towards the wood. 'Isandro is there with him. We've got to stop them fighting. I'm sure the other man knows more about fighting than Isandro does.'

Jaime rushed inside and came out with an old-fashioned hunting gun. Checking it, he hurried around the corner with Anna and his excited dog at his heels.

They reached the clearing and found it empty except for Isandro. He lay on the ground, a nasty cut on his head and blood trickling from his temple. The weapon, a stump of wood, lay nearby. She fell to her knees and felt his wrist for his pulse. She could feel the beat, even if it seemed a little irregular.

'Is he alright?'

'I think so, but he's unconscious. We'll have to get him back to the house somehow.' She looked around. That ruffian has gone.

Jaime looked around, the gun still in the crook of his elbow. 'Probably.' He pulled a big handkerchief from his pocket. 'Soak that in cold water, it might help to bring him round. You're within my sight, so nothing can happen. I can't understand why Pedro didn't bark. The only explanation I can think of is that the man made a wide detour around the back of the cottage, and was careful to remain out of sight and out of hearing, until he got to the wood.'

Anna soaked the handkerchief in cold water and brought it back. It did help. Isandro opened his eyes and struggled to a sitting position.

'Stay where you are for a moment. You took a nasty thump.'

Isandro put his hands on the side of his head. 'Yes. He hit me with that stump of wood before I even noticed he had it in his hands.'

With Jaime's help, he got groggily to his feet. He hung his arms around both their shoulders. They walked straight through the waters of the stream and when they reached the front of the cottage, Isandro leaned his head against the stonework and closed his eyes.

'Sit down, lad.' Jaime laid the gun aside and went indoors.

Worried, she watched and wondered what to do next.

Jaime returned with a towel and a tumbler. He handed Anna the towel. 'Soak that in the stream. It's not likely that villain is still around.' He turned to

Isandro. 'Here, drink a little cognac. It might help.'

Isandro sat on the bench and obeyed. Anna went off to soak the towel in the cold water. She returned and folded it to hold it against his head, but he took it from her and did it himself.

* * *

They heard the sound of a car engine in the distance and recognized the police. The wheels skidded in the dust as it drew up outside the cottage. When he got out, the detective in charge took one look at Isandro, and swore under his breath. 'Don't tell me. We're too late, aren't we?'

He listened to Isandro's account and viewed his bruised forehead. Using the car's radio, he requested medical help. The two policemen then set off in the direction of the wood. They told Jaime they hadn't seen any strange vehicle on their way to the cottage, so there was a chance he was still hiding somewhere nearby.

Anna and Jaime persuaded Isandro to lie down on the couch. He protested, but moved indoors. He looked relieved when he reached the couch.

Desperate to have something to do, she said, 'Let me soak the towel again.' She held out her hand.

His voice was as dogged as ever. 'Don't fuss, Anna!'

She gave him a hostile glare. 'I am not fussing! You're being stupid.'

'Oh, bloody hell!'

Jaime, standing in the background, chuckled. 'There's no point in arguing with a woman. Give her the towel!'

Isandro did, but scowled as he did so.

She marched to the door with it dangling from her hand.

★ ★ ★

Anna wished they were closer to medical help. On her return, Isandro

253

accepted the cold towel without comment.

Isandro closed his eyes. Jaime and Anna sat and waited silently. After a while, Jaime got up and made them some coffee. Anna's nervousness increased. Isandro wouldn't lie there so quiet and unresponsive unless he was feeling really bad.

Daylight gradually faded. The detectives returned and they had some good news. They'd cornered and then caught the burglar.

'He tried to hide between outcrops of rocks on the other side of the wood. He was avoiding coming back in the direction of the cottage in case he ran into more opposition again. He isn't dressed or equipped to go over THE nearest mountains so I expect he intended to wait for the cover of darkness to creep back to his car, wherever he left it. He didn't reckon with us turning up, or that we would search for him.'

Jaime asked, 'Where's his car? He

couldn't have got here without one.'

'He probably parked it off the track somewhere out of sight, between here and the road. We'll search for it tomorrow when it gets light. Most likely, he followed Señor Rodriguez, hoping he'd lead him to Miss Coleman. He figured there must be a connection, and decided it was worth a try to find her.'

Anna asked, 'Why go to all that trouble?'

He shrugged. 'In all probability, to put the fear of god into you. If you identified him in court, he'd end up with a prison sentence. We've locked him in our car. My colleague and he are handcuffed together so there is no chance of him escaping. We'll charge him with breaking and entering, threatening behaviour and causing bodily harm. We'll take him back to Lleida now. You can sleep easy, Miss Coleman. How do you feel, Señor Rodriguez?'

Isandro sat up. His face was ashen and his dark eyes looked dull.

255

Without waiting for his reply, the detective continued. 'I did request for medical help, but they just told us they have difficulty in finding the right place to turn off the road. I can understand that. It's not easy in daylight, and now that it is dark, it's almost impossible.' He paused. 'I think the best solution would be for you to come with us and we'll take you to the hospital. You ought to see a doctor.'

Isandro lifted his hand in protest, but before he could say a word, Anna said, 'That's an excellent idea.'

Jaime nodded. 'I think so too.'

'I'm fine. Stop making such a fuss!'

Anna snapped at him. 'I don't know if you've thought about the possibility that you have concussion or some other kind of brain damage? You need to check if anything serious has happened.'

He glowered and looked away. 'Okay! Okay! If it keeps everyone happy!'

Anna didn't care about his bad temper as long as he went to hospital.

The police officer addressed Isandro. 'I'll drive as carefully as possible. It really is the most sensible thing for you to do, señor.'

* * *

Isandro settled into the passenger seat in the front of the police car. Anna and Jaime watched. Anna avoided looking in the back where the assistant-detective sat securely handcuffed to the burglar.

Before the detective got in, he said, 'I'll need an official statement from you, Miss Coleman. When you visit Señor Rodriguez, please call at headquarters and ask for me, or my assistant.'

She nodded and stood next to Jaime. Isandro didn't look well but he managed a tight-lipped smile when the engine sprang to life. They drove off, and she and Jaime stood watching until the red tail-lights were two small pinpoints in the distance.

* * *

Finally, Jaime put his arm round her cold shoulder and directed her indoors. He put a match to the wood in the cast-iron stove and it brought some life to her body. Did she feel cold because of the outside temperatures, or because of this afternoon's happenings? Jaime insisted she drank a little cognac. It helped to put some warmth back into her and they turned their attention to making the evening meal. Anna wasn't hungry but it kept her hands busy and forced her to think of something else besides the results of Isandro's examination in hospital.

* * *

She hardly slept. She tossed and turned and thought about Isandro in Lleida. She felt terrible. His injury was her fault but it wasn't just that fact that bothered her so much. She'd never cared for someone so much before. He meant more to her than her own life and she was frightened for him.

When she entered the small living room early next morning, she stoked the fire in the stove and put the kettle on to make their morning coffee. She was glad to have something to do. They shared their simple breakfast, and although Jaime gave her a reassuring smile, neither of them talked much.

Finally, Jaime looked across the simple wooden table and said, 'We'll go into Lleida straight after breakfast, okay?'

Anna nodded.

Studying her, Jaime decided her concern for him was more than sheer friendship. He hoped she wouldn't be left disillusioned and devastated.

Before leaving, he ordered Pedro to guard the house. The dog's eyes pleaded but he obeyed and lay down across the entrance with his head on his paws.

★ ★ ★

In Lleida, they went straight to the hospital. Jaime enquired where they could find Isandro. The man checked the list of recent admittances and told him which level, and which room.

Jaime said, 'I'm going to see if I can talk to a doctor. Go ahead. I'll join you as soon as I find someone to give me some details.'

Anna went towards the lift. She pressed the button for the fourth floor. When the doors slid open, she only hoped with all her heart to find him feeling a lot better. She started down the corridor checking the room numbers. Her steps faltered when she saw Maria coming towards her.

They met halfway. Maria stood with one hand on her hip and said sarcastically, 'Now look who's here! If it isn't Miss Catastrophe herself! What are you doing here? Haven't you caused enough trouble already?'

She forced herself to be calm. 'Hello, Maria. How's Isandro?'

Reluctantly, she uttered between thin

lips, 'He's feeling a little better this morning, but that's no thanks to you.'

Anna ignored the attack. She was too curious not to ask. 'How did you know he was here?'

Condescendingly, she replied, 'I phoned him last night. He was admitted with his phone in his pocket. After they completed their examinations, they gave him a sedative. The night nurse heard his phone ringing in the drawer by his bedside and she answered it. She told me what had happened and I came straight away.'

Anna nodded. She stared at the other woman's flashing eyes. Maria clearly disliked her and she couldn't blame her. 'I didn't want it to happen, Maria. You must realize that. I'd never willingly put anyone in danger. Especially not Isandro; he has been extremely kind to me.'

'Huh! Then why do you cling to him like a limpet to a rock? He doesn't need you and he only helped you out of sheer charity. He pitied you, after that burglary, and he had a bad conscience because it all started after you stayed in *Casa Grande*. Why don't you just go home and stay out of his life from now on?'

Tears burned at the back of Anna's eyes. Somehow, she kept them under control. 'I didn't want him to help me. It was his suggestion that I visited Jaime. How should I guess that man would still try to cause trouble? Once Isandro has made up his mind about something, nothing will stop him. You know that. He was kind to me and thoughtful. He wanted to make the rest of my stay easier. To make up for what happened at *Casa Grande* that night.'

Maria hissed through her teeth. 'Well now you can make up for everything that has happened to him by just going away. Your visit this morning is pointless. He needs peace and quiet and they are requirements you don't create. I've phoned his family and they're on the way. I don't imagine they will be very happy to see you. We are all the visitors he needs.'

'Did he suffer concussion? Is he all right? You can at least tell me that.'

Maria wrapped a finger around a strand of her hair and eyed her carefully but she gave Anna the information she needed. 'Apparently he had light concussion but there's no . . . what do call it in English . . . fracture. No lasting problems. He feels much better this morning, but the hospital will keep him under observation for a day or two. That was a nasty blow, and he's been lucky.'

'I know, and I'm terribly sorry it happened. Give him my best wishes.' She turned on her heel and went.

* * *

Anna waited downstairs in the reception area, staring unseeingly out of the window at the traffic outside. Jaime returned from wherever he'd been and found her waiting.

'What are you doing here? Didn't you find him?'

She swallowed a lump in her throat and tried to sound casual. 'I met Maria in the corridor. She doesn't think it's a good idea for us to visit Isandro this morning. She did say he is better and there's no permanent damage. That's the main thing. Did you find someone to talk to?'

'Maria? How the hell did she get here so fast? Yes, I spoke to someone. He couldn't officially tell me anything, but he said there's no danger. Isandro will remain under observation for a day or two. He still has a whopping headache, but that's nothing unusual under the circumstances. They gave him sedation last night. He wanted to leave, after they confirmed there were no serious injuries.'

With difficulty, Anna laughed softly. 'Typical. If we can't visit him, can we go to the police station now and get the formalities out of the way?'

He looked at her pale face and the sadness in her eyes. 'Yes, of course. We can try to see him another time. Let's go.' He tucked her arm through his.

★ ★ ★

Jaime translated and the detective took her statement about what happened.

Anna asked, 'Will I have to appear personally in court? I'm going home to the UK soon and if I need to return to give evidence, it might be difficult for me to get leave. I'll need special permission and I know that my headmaster won't be very happy to agree.'

'It takes time for things to get to court. Señor Rodriguez is here and will be able to give evidence. Your written statement may be acceptable, under the circumstances, but I can't guarantee that. Have you seen him this morning? How is he?'

Jaime said, 'Better, but still in hospital.'

The detective nodded. 'We've already started checking. It looks likes like this chap and his brother are responsible for

265

several break-ins along the coast. He recognised you when he was on the road to Lleida. It was a chance meeting. He hoped to scare you. He admitted to trying to frighten you by pushing your car off the road, although he said he didn't intend injuring you seriously. It was an impulsive act and when he had time to think about it, he felt even more desperate. You'd seen him for a second time. His one source was Señor Rodriguez, and he started following him when he found you'd checked out of the hotel and driven off somewhere with him. He believed it was a stroke of luck to find you alone in the wood, and says he wanted to scare you so much that you wouldn't give evidence against him in court. He didn't see Señor Rodriguez was in the wood. He thought you were alone and it would be easy to bully you into silence. He panicked when they came face to face. He's a nasty piece of humanity. The two brothers have been in trouble for years for petty crimes. Until now they had no record of violence.' He added, 'They live near Lleida. His brother turned out to be an easier nut to crack. When we put the pressure on him he admitted everything. We even found some of the stolen goods in his flat today. They held on to items for a while before trying to sell them. I think Señor Rodriguez's property is among the items we found.'

Anna couldn't help asking, 'Was the Picasso sketch there too?'

'I can't say for sure, but I think so.'

18

Back at the cottage, Anna relaxed a little now she knew Isandro was on the mend. Anna didn't mind going back to the wood on her own to look for her satchel either. The wrongdoer was behind bars. The wood was a cathedral of green. The wind rustling the leaves was the only sound. She wove her way along the familiar route between the knotted trunks of the trees again, and found her satchel easily. Walking back slowly to Jaime, Anna decided it was time to move out.

They prepared their evening meal together as usual. They washed up and relaxed in their respective armchairs each side of the oven afterwards. Anna looked sideways at Isandro's car keys in a blue ceramic bowl on the table.

'I think it is time for me to end my visit, Jaime. We heard this morning that

Isandro will be in hospital for a day or two more. He won't need his jeep for a couple of days. When I met her in the hospital Maria told me his parents were on the way, so he'll probably go home with them, or even go to Barcelona with Maria. It was almost time for me to leave anyway. I can drive the jeep back to *Casa Grande* for him, and provide myself with transport to St. Sabatien at the same time.'

He leaned forward and the dying sunlight from one of the small windows threw a gentle glow across his tanned features. 'I'll drive you back when the time comes.'

She locked her ankles and wrung her hands briefly. 'You'd have to drive me there, and then drive all the way back. It would take you most of the day. It would also be a waste of petrol. I think everyone will persuade him not to come here straight from the hospital.' She thought about Isandro and Maria together in Barcelona and it left a bitter taste in her throat.

'Don't you want to go to the hospital again to see him before you leave?'

She shook her head determinedly. 'Maria said I bring him bad luck. Maybe she's right. I'll leave him a note.'

'That's silly. You don't bring anyone bad luck. You're the one who's had bad luck. Don't listen to Maria. She overestimates her own importance. She may be a TV presenter but that doesn't mean she talks sense. Wait a bit longer.'

She shook her head, got up and reached for the keys. 'There's no point in waiting. I'll practise driving the jeep for a little before the daylight fades completely. I've never driven a four wheel drive, is it difficult?'

* * *

Jaime knew he'd miss her. She'd been an undemanding guest. A gut feeling told him something was fundamentally wrong. She was trying to avoid another meeting with Isandro. He couldn't give her any other reason to delay her departure, because he didn't know what Isandro felt about Anna. He couldn't stop her and he couldn't tell her what she should, or shouldn't do. She'd go her own way. She was a placid character but a determined one, someone who knew her own mind.

Next morning, Anna's eyes were moist when she kissed his leathery cheek. 'Thank you for having me. How do people keep in touch with you? I'd like to send you a note now and then if I may?'

'You do that. I'd like to keep in contact.' He gave her a hug. 'I have a post-box number in Lleida. Wait a minute; I'll write it down for you. Let me know how you are, and come back again to visit me — any time.'

She took the piece of paper and smiled. 'Perhaps I'll do that. I loved it here. Take care, Jaime!'

'I will. I'm already missing you.'

She started the engine. It felt strange to drive Isandro's jeep. It was very different in shape and size to the cars

271

she'd driven, but she managed. As she drove off towards the road, she waved her hand above her head and beeped the horn several times. She checked the rear mirror and saw him standing with the dog, and watching her. It was poignant to see him standing there on his own. Her eyes were misty. She followed the bumpy track back to the main road and went straight on without stopping until she reached St. Sabatien.

* * *

When she arrived, her plans gradually began to fall into place easier than she expected. She drove to the hotel first and parked around the corner. Señora Mendora bustled around her and greeted her effusively. Anna decided not to mention what had happened. If she did, Anna wouldn't be able to get away until she gave her a detailed description. Señora Mendora did have one important message, from the car-hire company. They'd parked a replacement car on the slope behind the hotel and Señora Mendora had the keys. Anna's problem about getting to the airport dissolved into thin air. Now she only needed an earlier flight. She wanted to leave as soon as possible, even if that meant buying a second, new return ticket.

Anna borrowed some hotel stationery and, in the silence of her bedroom, she wrote Isandro her note. She wrote several versions before she thought that she'd got it right.

Dear Isandro,

Thank you for all your help and your hospitality. I hope that you're fully recovered by the time you read this. Jaime promised me he'd explain why I drove your jeep home. I thought your parents might take you straight back to St. Sabatien, or that you'd go to Barcelona with Maria. Either way, it would be complicated for you to pick up the jeep from Jaime. Someone would have to take you there. I decided if I left the jeep at Casa Grande it would help solve a problem for you. It also solved my problem of getting back to the hotel without involving Jaime.

I've decided to go back to the UK straight away. School starts soon, and the police assured me that if they want me for any reason now, or in the future, they know where I am and will get in touch. I'll use the remaining holiday to catch up on all the various tasks I've been putting off, but which need to be done.

I wish you all the luck in the world for your professional and personal future. I'll always remember my holiday in St. Sabatien. I'm sorry I caused you so much trouble.

Next time you speak to Teresa, please tell her I'll be in touch when school has settled into a routine. Best wishes, and take care of you, and yours. Anna

Leaving the jeep parked in the court-yard, she pushed her message and the keys of the jeep into the letterbox. She didn't yield to the temptation to linger and she didn't look back towards the entrance once she began to walk back towards the small village. Her throat tightened and her eyes misted with unshed tears when she realized she'd broken the final ties with Isandro. Back in the hotel, she phoned Jaime's friend in Lleida. She asked him to tell Jaime that she'd arrived safely. He didn't speak much English but enough to understand he should tell Jaime that someone called Anna had reached St. Sabatien unharmed.

★　★　★

There were no seats free when she contacted the airline next morning. She asked them to add her name to the waiting list and decided to wait at least another day before thinking about an alternative route home. In the end, someone cancelled their flight for the following day and Anna packed her suitcases.

She felt nostalgic as she took a final walk around the harbour, and along the sand. She went as far as his sign asking people not to trespass on private property. She ran her hand across the black lettering before she turned back. She'd was determined never return to the small village.

★ ★ ★

She said goodbye to the Mendoras and thanked them for everything. She left for Barcelona in plenty of time and returned the car to the hire company. She waited calmly until her flight call.

★ ★ ★

Hours later, her shoes sounded hollow as she went down the steps to her basement flat. She ruffled in her bag for her keys and went inside. The narrow hallway had a former pantry and her bedroom on one side, and the kitchen and bathroom on the other. The square-shaped living room was at the end of the corridor and was the largest room in the flat. Passing through it, Anna unlocked the door to the patio and let fresh air invade the rooms. She noticed her neighbour had kept her plants supplied with water.

She turned and considered her flat; she liked it. It didn't compare to Isandro's house but she'd made the best out of its possibilities. It looked cozy and attractive. She'd chosen light colours to compensate for the lack of natural lighting. Pine bookcases lined the walls filled with countless books. The settee and easy chairs were cream with multi-hued cushions tucked into their corners. A dining table stood on a rush carpet near the patio window; its matching chairs were tucked neatly out of sight underneath. The afternoon sunshine spilled through the rear windows and made moving patterns on the wood.

She could have afforded a bigger flat, at road level, but Anna remained where she was. Partly because it had taken her a long time to decorate it properly, and partly because she wanted to save for her own flat, or house, one day.

Anna went back for her suitcases, and humped them into her bedroom. A faint smell of geraniums and myrtle invaded the rooms from the patio. She opened a bottle of white wine, from a small sideboard, and poured herself a glass. She took it outside, sat on one of the wrought iron chairs and hoisted her legs onto the other. Looking back, the holiday now seemed to be a dream. She'd expected to spend a quiet relaxing holiday, but it had turned out to be unforgettable, in more senses than one. She'd faced some uncomfortable experiences but she'd also met her dream man.

Smoothing her hair back off her face, she took a sip of the wine and decided action and work was one way to cope. Leaving the wine glass in the kitchen, she began to unpack the suitcases. Soon the washing machine hummed and her bags were back in their usual position on the top shelf in the pantry. Grabbing her car keys, she set off to replenish the fridge. Perhaps she should phone one of her friends later, and arrange to meet for a coffee in town soon. She wasn't strong enough to talk about Isandro to anyone yet, but there was always plenty to chat about and she was a good listener.

She tried desperately to occupy herself. Unable to sleep properly, she was determined not to give in to her longing to break down and cry. Acting defiantly got her from one day to the next, but it didn't stop her thinking about him all the time. When she started back to school the following Monday, she had never had such an orderly household and she'd even repainted her bedroom; something she'd been putting off for months. The flat shone, and her chores were all up to date.

★ ★ ★

She loved her job. This term she felt particularly glad to be back at school. The first few days were always busy ones for teachers and pupils. Anna didn't mind. It helped to fill some of the gaps inside.

Everyone was still fresh and relaxed when they met up on the first day. She got on with nearly all the others but not with the deputy head. Most of the staff didn't get on with him either. They all agreed that as he'd be retiring in two years' time, it would be best to put up with him until then. They all tried to cushion the effects of his old-fashioned, strict regulations. Back in the classroom, she enjoyed being with her class again; she'd missed them. Their never-ending stories about where they'd been and what they saw on holiday made it all worthwhile. It took a couple of days until the children and the school settled down after the summer holidays, but gradually they agreed the timetables, accepted the duty rotas and routine took over again.

Other teachers told about their experiences in an assortment of holiday destinations and the positive and negative incidents. Anna didn't talk much about Spain. It hurt to talk about the places and people she'd grown to like and to love. It wakened memories of what might have been. She just said she'd had a great time, met some nice people, and enjoyed herself very much. No one noticed that Anna didn't offer as much information as usual.

19

In the middle of preparing her evening meal, a knock on the door interrupted her. She didn't expect any visitor. Checking through the peephole, the breath caught in her throat when she saw it was Isandro. Trying to normalize the racing of her heart, she took a deep breath, opened the door, and smiled.

'Isandro! What a surprise.'

He eyed her purposefully. Her heart thundered and Anna only realized how much she'd missed seeing him. She longed to touch him. She inhaled the familiar smell of whatever woody soap or after-shave he used and felt light-headed. She was still sensible enough to add, 'Please come in. What are you doing here? How do you know where I live?'

He ducked his head and entered. The soft folds of his coat brushed her as he entered the hallway. As soon as she closed the door, he reached out and pulled her roughly into his arms. The minute he held her, his mouth covered hers hungrily. Her own eager response shocked her. She thought she'd be able to control her feelings. His kiss sent the pit of her stomach into a wild swirl. She felt vulnerable and shivers of desire also raced through her and made her powerless to resist. His lips were delicious and she savoured every moment. Her knees weakened and she tried hard to remain level-headed. It didn't work. Her heartbeat thundered faster and was completely out of control. Using the palms of her hands to free herself, she stopped him kissing her, but he held onto her snugly. He smiled instead, and her pulses raced even faster.

His dark eyebrows lifted and he said dryly, 'I've come to see you — that's obvious, isn't it? The visiting card you gave me for the car-hire company told me all I needed to know.

He was too close for comfort. She saw the vestiges of the bruises on the side of his head and longed to touch them. She felt the hard contours of his body. She longed to just enjoy him, it what she'd dreamed about, but her ideas were stupid. Looking up into his dark eyes, she managed to stutter, 'It still doesn't explain why you've come. I thought I'd sorted everything out. Didn't you get my note?' Anna wished she could ask him why he held her as if he'd never let go again; she didn't, because it felt too good to be in his arms.

He looked around briefly and took in his surroundings. 'Umm! Nice. I like it.'

'I'm glad you approve.'

He had a girlfriend, she'd never encouraged him, and he'd never implied he even liked her much, apart from one brief kiss. Why had he come all this way? She resolved to mention all of that in a moment when he loosened his grip and gave her a chance to get her emotions under control again. She hoped he didn't notice what a devastating effect he had on her. Perhaps this was a game. Perhaps he'd noticed she loved him and he presumed she'd agree to an affair. Well he'd be disappointed, however much she loved him.

Without loosening his hold, he began to shuffle her along in a chasse movement. The effect of their bodies moving in a slow rhythm felt almost unbearable. She ran her tongue over her lips and he followed the movement with his eyes and his face creased into a knowing smile. Once they'd reached the living room, he stopped and despite all her resolve, they both smiled simultaneously. Anna knew she ought to keep him at bay, but she failed miserably.

He uttered, 'Where were we? Oh yes, your fantastic little note in my letterbox. We ought to clear that out of the way first. It didn't explain why you disappeared without visiting me in hospital. You were the one who insisted I went there.'

'I . . . I had to leave. My holiday was ending and I had to come back, you know that. School began this week.' She needed time to adjust to his being here in her flat, and of her still being in his arms.

His laugh was low and throaty. 'You still had more than a week of your holiday left when we last saw each other. You left me lying in that hospital and didn't come to see me. Not once.'

She managed to wriggle her way out of his arms so that she could think more clearly. 'Oh, hospital! Yes! How are you? No after-effects; I hope?'

'You're the only after-effect I know about.'

'Me?' Her voice sounded squeaky. She cleared her throat. Looking at his expression, her heart missed a few beats before her pulse starting pounding crazily. 'Because it was my fault you ended up in hospital? Yes, I'm sorry. If I could have stopped that man clubbing you, I would have, of course. Perhaps a combined effort would have driven him off.'

Sounding slightly exasperated, he replied, 'I'm not talking about the attack, or why I was in hospital. I want to know why you left me without saying goodbye. You didn't give me a chance to straighten things between us — and we have to do that, don't we?' He took a step forward; Anna stepped back, and hid her hands behind her. Her body craved for the feel of his hands. That was madness.

Thinking it might be better for her to look irritated, Anna retorted, 'Jaime and I came to the hospital, to see you. Maria stopped me visiting and told me to leave. I didn't think you wanted to see me after that. I told her to give you my best wishes.'

He looked surprised and exasperated. 'Maria sent you away, and you went away without checking if she was telling the truth? Jaime said you came with him to visit me, but he didn't know exactly what Maria said to you, just that it was better for you not to visit me. I didn't know that Maria had interfered. I waited for you to visit me. Day after day.' He ran his hand through his black hair; it sprang back into position. 'Jaime came to see me a day after you'd left him. I was hoping both of you had come to collect me, but when he told me you'd left, I was shocked. I didn't explain why, that would have given the game away, and I didn't want to talk to anyone else about us until I'd talked to you first. He's a wily old fox; I'm sure he guessed why I was so surprised and mad. Surely, you realize I'd have hopped out of bed and grabbed you if I'd only known you were outside in the corridor. I was just lying there wondering if I meant anything to you at all. Do I matter to you?'

Flustered by his words, she crossed her arms, coloured, and said pointedly, 'I met Maria on the way to your room. She's your girlfriend, and she more or less told me to leave. She had every right to do so. She said I'd brought you nothing but bad luck ever since we met.' The colour increased when she added, 'By the way, I don't think she'd approve of you kissing me like you did just now; and I don't either. I don't like messing around with other women's boyfriends, you know that.'

'You don't like kissing me? That's not the impression I got a minute ago.'

She looked at him silently.

He ran his hands through his thick black hair and it sprang back into place. 'My dear heart, Maria and I are through with each other, and have been for weeks, ever since the morning after the burglary. I suddenly realized I didn't like her much. She's intelligent, she's pretty, but she's like a jagged iceberg if anyone gets in the way of her plans and ambitions. She had absolutely no right to stop you visiting me and I don't know why she did so. As to you bringing me bad luck, you're the best thing that's ever happened to me.'

She blinked and listened in bewilderment. 'You and Maria are . . . ?'

He nodded and reached out. She

didn't resist anymore.

'Whatever it was, it's over and ended! I've been waiting for this moment to explain to you for ages. I couldn't understand myself, or my feelings, at first. Initially, you were just a summer tourist. Then you were Teresa's new friend. Suddenly, you filled my thoughts every day. I gradually began to notice I felt about you in a way I'd never experienced before. When that idiot pushed you off the road, you can't imagine how angry and frightened I was. I suddenly realized I loved you. I wanted to protect you from harm, and up until then I hadn't even kissed you!'

She caught her breath and thoughts and feelings tumbled and assailed her. She found it hard to remain coherent when he was so close. 'Why was Maria in the hospital when I arrived? she said she'd been there since the previous evening. She must have broken all the speed limits to get to you as fast as she could. She wouldn't have done that unless she thought that you wanted her.'

He shrugged. 'I was already sleeping when she turned up; I don't know what she told the hospital authorities. Perhaps she blinded them with the knowledge they were dealing with a television celebrity. They gave me sedation to keep me quiet and to stop me jumping out of bed. Perhaps she hoped to change my mind by showing some concern. Apparently, she phoned me on impulse. She didn't have a partner to go to some important party or other. A night nurse answered the phone to stop it disturbing the other patients.' He shrugged. 'I considered asking her about her motives for coming but I realized I didn't care, whatever they were, so I never bothered. I just told her I felt nil and zero for her.'

Anna's eyes brightened with anticipation and he longed to disregard any further explanations, but she needed to know, so he continued.

'She told her boss that she'd had a

tip about important news breaking in Lleida and he allowed her to use the company helicopter. I can't imagine how she'll explain her way out of that, but I don't care. I tried not to sound too damning but told her we didn't suit and never had. She went off in a temper, cursing you and me. I continued to wait another day, for a visitor who never came. I wanted to find out if you felt something for me and if we had a chance of a future together, or not. I began to want you very badly on the day that I saw you with your boyfriend in the hotel. After that, the longings just grew. Someone tried to harm you and then they tried to harm me, and something seems to get in the way all the time.'

'My boyfriend?' Puzzled for a moment, she then said, 'Oh . . . you mean Mike? He's a colleague of mine. He intended to visit his girlfriend staying near Gerona and he called on the way.'

He nodded. 'How was I supposed to know that? Later you did mention he was a colleague, but when I saw you together that first time, I just presumed you were more than friends. I've never felt so jealous.'

Her mind reeled. 'Mike and I are friends, nothing more.' Her eyes widened. 'Does that mean you want us to be more than friends?'

He grinned wickedly. 'And how! My hopes are growing! That kiss a minute ago told me so but I want more, a lot more than a kiss. I didn't even understand why I didn't like Franco flirting with you; I'd never cared in that way before. Then Mike seemed to upset the apple cart, until you straightened that out for me. I still wondered if you had someone else waiting at home, when you didn't visit me in hospital. I had to know the truth. I don't intend to let you escape me again. Come here, Anna; come to my arms where you belong.' He looked her over seductively. 'Or do you have someone else after all? I won't give up without a fight.'

When their eyes met, her heart

turned over. She shook her head like a robot. 'Of course not. Don't be silly. I love you like crazy.' Standing on tiptoe, she touched her lips to his and then viewed him expectantly.

He chuckled, looked triumphant, and waited.

'This is completely mad. We live in two different countries. How do we know if we feel something serious that will last? Perhaps it'll die a quick death. That's the kind of relationship I never wanted. You know that.'

He nodded and remarked, 'But you want to give us a chance?'

She nodded dumbly.

'Good! That means you think I'm worth the risk.' He smiled and she couldn't resist him: she smiled back. He continued, 'Where there's a will, there's a way. I'm here and that's the start. I've got to be back for the final round of discussions about that museum complex next week, but we can talk every day on Skype, we can travel back and forth on cheap flights at the weekend, and we can be together at Christmas. That's not far off. You get a long holiday then. It'll be a perfect chance for you to meet my parents again. They liked you and they didn't like Maria after her performance that day. They'd never met her before. Teresa will be in Washington by Christmas, but Franco will probably parade his latest girlfriend in front of my parents, and I'll parade mine! Perhaps we should just consider the time in-between as a kind of testing time. If we love each other, and I really think we do, time will tell. We'll find a way round any difficulties that crop up. Love will find a way.'

Anna continued to nod and listen.

'We need to decide where we'll want to build our lives together. If you're prepared to come to Spain, I'm sure there are international schools in Barcelona where you could teach. You can think seriously about your dream to be a book illustrator. I'll do all I can to support you in any way I can. If my work continues to expand, you can take over the administrative side of things if you like. But, if you want to stay in the UK, it might make things more complicated work-wise for me, because my clients are all in Spain at present, but if you want to stay here, I'll move.'

She'd already made up her mind, but it showed her how much he loved her. 'And *Casa Grande*?'

He laughed softly. 'It's yours. It's ours. I'll never sell it, no matter what happens. It brought us together and I'm eternally grateful for that.' He considered her carefully. He said slowly and very seriously, searching for the right words, 'I didn't realize anything was missing in my life until I met you. I've family and friends, but when you came along that wasn't enough anymore. I want to be with you and spend the rest of my life making you happy, if I can. You can't change the past, but you can choose the present.'

'You came through my door a moment ago and you've already made my dreams come true.' She was powerless to resist him and she tingled under his fingertips.

She wondered if their meeting had been by chance. She thought about Jaime and remembered how love had come to him and his wife. Now it had happened to her and Isandro, not in exactly the same way, but their love was just as good. She didn't have time to sort out all her thoughts before his lips brushed hers again and she was lost.

His eyes were warm and Anna knew she made him happy. She automatically twined her arms round his neck and he deepened his kiss. He kissed her, and kissed her again, until her head spun, but she still longed for more. She had a white-hot desire in her blood and she looked at Isandro and knew he understood. No one else would ever make her feel like this. This man with his dark eyes and olive skin, his determination and his kindness — he was the one for Anna Coleman.

The late afternoon sunshine cast a glow across her small sitting room. He smiled at her as he guessed her deepest longings. 'I've waited too long, and so have you. Let's start getting to know each other properly.'

They still had all the details to settle, but it could wait for a while. Here and now was more important. He divested himself of his overcoat and her colour heightened. She reached out. An irresistible smile filled his face when he realized where they were heading.

'You're a woman after my heart, and I think you won it the day we met, even though we got off on the wrong foot. I know now my place is with you, always.' Anna thanked heaven that they had this weekend together, though she also knew the time ahead would be challenging and sometimes hard, but they'd manage and they'd find a way. She couldn't live without him. He'd said he loved her and needed her with him always, and she already knew Isandro never said anything he didn't mean.

SPECIAL MESSAGE TO READERS

THE ULVERSCROFT FOUNDATION
(registered UK charity number 264873)

was established in 1972 to provide funds for
research, diagnosis and treatment of eye diseases.
Examples of major projects funded by
the Ulverscroft Foundation are:-

- The Children's Eye Unit at Moorfields Eye Hospital, London
- The Ulverscroft Children's Eye Unit at Great Ormond Street Hospital for Sick Children
- Funding research into eye diseases and treatment at the Department of Ophthalmology, University of Leicester
- The Ulverscroft Vision Research Group, Institute of Child Health
- Twin operating theatres at the Western Ophthalmic Hospital, London
- The Chair of Ophthalmology at the Royal Australian College of Ophthalmologists

You can help further the work of the Foundation
by making a donation or leaving a legacy.
Every contribution is gratefully received. If you
would like to help support the Foundation or
require further information, please contact:

THE ULVERSCROFT FOUNDATION
The Green, Bradgate Road, Anstey
Leicester LE7 7FU, England
Tel: (0116) 236 4325

website: www.foundation.ulverscroft.com